Going All Out III

Written by

Dorian Sykes

RJ Publications, LLC

Newark, New Jersey

D1603381

The characters and events in this book are fictitious. Any resemblance to actual persons, living or dead is purely coincidental.

RJ Publications

www.rjpublications.com
Copyright © 2012 by RJ Publications
All Rights Reserved
ISBN-10: 1939284007
ISBN-13: 9781939284006

Printed in the United States

December 2012

1 2 3 4 5 6 7 8 9 10

Doubt…

Without question we are enemies…

But I respect you, because you always bring your best fight

when trying to deter my stride to triumph.

Acknowledgements

To anyone who has ever inspired a thought of mine, knowingly or subconsciously, I thank you. It is you all who plant the necessary seeds in author's minds, which we eventually use in our stories.

To my father, Ronald Gibson- Wherever you are, I hope God is keeping a watchful eye over you. When the times... right, we'll cross paths.

Tobias Sykes, my little cousin who use to stand on the front porch and yell my name is search or me. You've grown into a mature young man, and I'm proud of you on the graduation! Big thangs poppin...

Mojo – What's good? We finally gettin' this thang off the ground. Keep pushin' your pen. Remember our pact, never let the ink dry...

Prologue

"But that's yo' mother. Do you love me, Tez?" Lil; One sat up to face Tez. She looked deep into his eyes, as he spoke.

"Of course I love you. But will I die for you? Hell nah. That shit goes for my mom, my kinds, yo' ass and anybody else. Cause ain't nobody gone die for me. I wouldn't even expect them to. But like I told you last night. I'ma make it even…" Tez turned to leave.

"Where are you going?"

The door slammed as Tez stepped into the hallway of the complex. He exited the building and walked to his Audi. He popped the locks, then climbed behind the wheel. Tez sparked another blunt as he cruised down Petersburg Blvd. He was on his way to Royal Oak, Michigan. He flipped through his CD case and pulled Biggie's 2nd LP out, 'Life after Death' disc two. He put the CD in and skipped to 'What's Beef?' He had to set the mood for what follows…

Tez pulled into Bald Hills private community of Royal Oak, Michigan. The Audi was engulfed by huge Oak trees which lined both sides of the street, as Tez drove down Naples St. He locked his eyes on a recently build snow white Colonial-style mansion just two properties to his right. Tez pulled into the driveway and parked behind the lavender 500 SL Mercedes that sat parked in front of the garage. Tez took a long pull from the L, then sat it in the ashtray. "Beef is when yo' mom's ain't safe up the street…" Tez sung along to the chorus. He cut the car off, then pushed the door opened.

Tez was no stranger to the mansion. He had ate dinner there on several occasins, and even spent a few holidays there. He walked around the side of the estate and grabbed the screen door handle to the greenhouse. Tez stepped inside the greenhouse and walked over to the door adjacent leading to the main house. He turned the knob and let himself in. Tez walked through the formal dining room and into the arcade room.

"Wha't up lil' man?" asked Tez.

"Uncle Tez!" the little boy ran over to Tez and jumped into his arms.

"Where's your grandma?" Tez asked, holding the boy in his arms.

"Up stair. You bring me anything?" asked the little boy.

"Of course, I did," Tez sat him down, then dug in his pocket and gave the boy two hundreds.

"Thank you, uncle Tez."

"Your welcome. Let me go see 'bout Grandma."

The little boy rushed back over to the Grand Theft Auto arcade game he'd been playing. Tez started up the marble staircase...

*****

"So, your just going to run for the rest of your life? It's not fair to Jr., you know... He's asking me about you more and more everyday..."

"Ma, I'm not going to run forever. I just have some things that must be taken care of before I face the music."

"You know your momma is not stupid. I know what's going on, and its truly a shame. But I understand. You do what you must, so we can be a family again..."

Tez pulled his 40 cal. from his waist and crept down the hall toward the master bedroom. He could hear his target's voice talking on the phone…

"Oh, my God!"

"Moma, what's wrong?" asked Pharaoh.

"Boom! Boom! Boom! Boom!"

"Moma!" He held the phone to his ear waiting for a response from Ma' Dukes.

"Moma!..."

Tez walked over and picked the phone up from the bed.

"Moma!..." yelled Pharaoh.

"What up doe," said Tez.

Pharaoh's heart sunk. He knew that voice from anywhere…

"Now we're even…" said Tez, then slammed the phone on the hook...

Chapter One

Pharaoh slowly lowered his cell phone to his side. He hit the end button with his thumb, but hadn't focused on the phone. He was staring off into space, as he stood beside Stacy on the balcony. Stacy heard Pharaoh yelling and got up from the brunch she and Pharaoh had been sharing. She had been repeatedly asking Pharaoh what was going on.

"Talk to me, baby, what's going on?" Stacy tugged at Pharaoh's arm trying to break his trance.

Pharaoh was lost in disbelief. All sorts of questions ran through his mind. 'Was that really Tez? Did this nigga just shoot my moma? Is she dead?' Pharaoh thought. He continued in his trance, not answering Stacy. She followed him through the sliding patio door into the master bedroom.

"Pharaoh, you're scaring me. Please talk to me," Stacy pleaded. She followed Pharaoh into the walk-in closet where he kneeled to the floor and began stuffing clothes inside two Louis Vutton luggages. He zipped the bags shut, then carried them into the bedroom tossing them on the bed. Stacy folded her arms and stepped back, while she watched Pharaoh empty the top dresser drawer where he kept loose money. He emptied the drawer into a Stacy Adams shoe box, and then scanned the room. "Come on, we're leaving," Pharaoh said, finally breaking his silence, but not his trance. He grabbed the two Louis V bags and the bag with the loose cash and headed for the staircase.

"I wish you'd tell me what's wrong," Stacy said, following Pharaoh down the spiral steps.

Pharaoh took one last look at the living room before snatching the front door open. "Open the trunk," he ordered walking around Stacy's side of her Durango.

Stacy hit the button on her key chain, and Pharaoh raised the hatch up. He stuffed the bag of money under the spare tire and tossed the luggage bags over it.

"Let's go," he said walking around to the passenger door.

Stacy reluctantly climbed behind the wheel. She sat there with her arms folded refusing to start the truck.

"What are you doin'?" Pharaoh turned and asked Stacy. "Start the truck and let's go…"

"Go where, Pharaoh? Why don't you just tell me what's going on…"

"Look, just start the fuckin' truck and let's go!" yelled Pharaoh.

Stacy had never once seen Pharaoh lose his cool. He was hysterical. Stacy stuck the key in the ignition and started the truck. She periodically looked over at Pharaoh as they drove along the shoreline of the Detroit River. Pharaoh was calling every number he knew, which was slim to none. He started with Ralph, but the phone kept going to voicemail. He started to try and call his brother Donald, but he knew that the feds were still tracking him, figuring Donald would lead them to him. "Fuck…" Pharaoh closed the cell phone shut and leaned his head back against the headrest.

Stacy was pulling up to the bridge, and Pharaoh's stomach did a flip at the sight of the border patrol agent. He carefully slid his seat belt across his lap, and fastened it. The white agent flagged Stacy to pull over…

'Shit,' thought Pharaoh.

Stacy pulled over in front of the small station and the border agent approached the driver's window, but hadn't taken his eyes off Pharaoh. Stacy popped straight into cop mode. She placed both hands on the steering wheel where the agent could see them.

"License, please," said the agent.

Pharaoh kept his head straight facing the bridge. He could feel the agent staring a hole through the side of his face. Stacy flipped the sun visor down and handed the agent her license, along with her Wayne County sheriff's badge. The agent's mood and detection lightened as he reviewed Stacy's credentials. He smiled, then handed Stacy back her license and badge. "Thank you. Have a nice day." The agent tapped the roof of the truck and Stacy pulled back onto the bridge.

Pharaoh's mind locked back on his mom. He let out a deep sigh as he held the phone to his ear... Ralph's voicemail angered Pharaoh. 'Where the fuck this lil' nigga at?' he thought. Stacy exited the Ambassador Bridge and turned down Jefferson Ave. Pharaoh peered out the window at all the hustling and bustling going down. Wino's decorated the exterior of Scotch Castles' Liquor Store on the corner of Grand Blvd. and Jefferson Ave. Pharaoh watched from the red light, as a red drop-top Camaro filled with young white chicks crossed onto the Belle Isle Bridge. Summer was still in full swing and Detroit was alive.

Pharaoh didn't plan on returning to the city until his 'hit list' was all taken care of, but the circumstances warranted his early return. He was hoping when he returned that everything could go back to normal... Pharaoh turned and met eyes with Stacy...."I guess you were right," he said then returned his stare back to the window.

"Right about what,Pharaoh?"

"Everything! Us having a happy ending and my plans being too far-fetched and me going back to jail..."

"What are you talkin' about? Please tell me what's going on," pleaded Stacy.

Pharaoh went back into his shell. He flipped his cell and tried calling Ralph one more time, but still got his voicemail. Pharaoh sat up in his seat and directed Stacy where to take him...

"Slow down," said Pharaoh as they rode pass the house on Rosemary. The house was boarded up and yellow crime tape stretched across the banister of the porch. The side of the house was partially burned, like someone threw a cocktail through the window...

'What the fuck?' thought Pharaoh. He sat back in his seat and tried to make sense of it all. 'Where the fuck is Ralph,' he thought.

"Where to now?" asked Stacy.

Pharaoh really didn't know. In essence, he didn't have anywhere to go, except back over to Canada, or Stacy's house. Neither one was an option.

"Take me to Al's Barber shop. It's on 7 Mile and Moenart." Pharaoh gave Stacy the directions and within minutes they were pulling in front of Al's place. Stacy parked behind the pearl white Lincoln Mark 8. Pharaoh knew the car from anywhere, it belonged to an old playa' named Teacher. Pharaoh looked around and saw all the major playas' cars...

E-major's Navigator, Rich-Bo's 500 SL' and Maurice's cocaine white 420 SL.

"Why do I get the feeling that this will be the last time I'll see you?" asked Stacy, as she cut the truck off.

Pharaoh faced Stacy then spoke, "I asked you a while ago if you thought what I was doing was far-fetched, and you said yes. I asked you whether you saw a future for us, and you wouldn't give me a straight answer…"

"Pharaoh…"

"No, let me finish. You didn't have to answer for me to understand. So, I'm not going to sit back and wait until I go to jail for you to leave me. You said let's just enjoy the time we have together. Well, it's been real." Pharaoh pulled on the door handle and got out the truck. He walked around back and pulled his hoody over his head, then raised the hatch to get his bag.

"So, you leaving me, after all I helped you through?" Stacy asked, crying.

Pharaoh pulled his bags out, and shut the hatch. "Look, Stacy, I will always have love for you, always. And maybe in the end we just might have our happy ending. But right now, it's good-bye." Pharaoh leaned in and kissed Stacy on the forehead, then wiped her tears from her face. "I love you," said Pharaoh, then turned and walked away. He walked around the side of Rockie's Beauty Salon adjacent to Al's and into the alley-way. Pharaoh dialed the number painted on the front of the building and waited by the back door as the phone began ringing.

Noise filled Pharaoh's receiver as Redman snatched the phone off the hook. "Al's…."

"Let me holla at Mo'."

"Maurice!" yelled Redman, as he stepped back into the crap game that was in full-swing.

"It's a bet, nigga. I'll be right back. Bo' let me know if he craps out. "Hello," said Maurice picking up the phone.

"Mo it's me, Pharaoh."

"What's up boy? I got a bone to pick with you. Where are you at?"

"Check this out, Mo, I'm outside in the back of the shop."

"Fuck you doin' back there?"

"I didn't want nobody seein' me. So, don't say nothin'. Just casually slide out and holla' at me."

'On my way." Click.

"Did he miss?" Maurice asked walking through the backroom.

"Nah, he made it," said Rich-Bo.

"Shit…" Mo' peeled off five hundred dollar bills, then tossed them dead center of the table.

"Where you going? Bet it back," said Fly-guy Willie.

Mo' tucked his bankroll in his pants pocket. "Nah, I gotta handle something, I'll be back though." Maurice cracked the back door and slid outside.

Pharaoh stood up from behind the grill and stepped around it to greet Mo.

"Boy, you betta be glad I love you cause you cost me some money in there. Come here and give me a hug," Mo smiled then opened his arms wide.

"Mo, I need your help," Pharaoh said, ending their embrace.

"You got that. But first, tell me what you were thinking havin' that boy's momma killed. I taught you better and that," said Mo with a look of disappointment,

"Who are you talkin' about?" asked Pharaoh.

"Tez. You had that lil' cat, what's his name. Damn, I hate it when I forget things. Anyway, he killed Brenda yesterday morning," said Mo'.

"What?"

"Yeah…Ralph, that's his name."

"What about Ralph?"

"He came to the shop yesterday claiming to be your lil' man, and he said that he was helping you with some thangs… You know, then he asked me where Tez's mother lived. I told him cause I figured he was gon' lay on the nigga."

Pharaoh dropped his head. " I can't believe this," he said.

"I thought you sent him to do that?"

"Mo, you know me better than that. But listen, it's done and not only that, Tez has done something in return to my mom's."

"Are you serious?"

"Yeah, but I don't know to what extent. I need you to put me up in a house somewhere and I need a car."

Mo dug in his pocket, then gave Pharaoh the keys to his 420SL Benz. "What about money, you straight on cash?" Mo asked, while digging in his other pocket.

Pharaoh stuck his hand out and slightly waved no. "I'm cool," he said raising the Stacy Adams bag.

"One of those keys is to a lil spot I got off Kelly Road. Right now I got my side-chick living there, her name is Token. She's a young broad but has real good manners."

"That's cool, Mo. I just need somewhere to lay my head," said Pharaoh.

"A'ight, well I'll call her and tell her you're on your way. I'll be over to check on you probably tomorrow." Mo gave, Pharaoh another hug then sent him off to his Benz.

Pharaoh threw his bags in the trunk, and then sunk into the tan butter soft leather seat. He backed away from Rich-Bo's 500 SL before pulling into traffic.

'That's why yo' lil' ass ain't picking up yo' phone, cause you know I'ma kill you,' thought Pharaoh. It was all starting to make sense...

Chapter Two

Token was standing on the small front porch facing Kelly Road. She was talking on the cordless phone to her girlfriend Princess, while waiting on Pharaoh to pull up. "I think this is him now. Hmm. He's fine. I'ma call you back," said Token.

She hit the off button and started down the stairs. Her titties bounced firmly with every step down she took, and her ass cheeks fought to stay inside the purple boy shorts she was wearing. Pharaoh pulled into the driveway and parked behind Token's silver Explorer. He cut the car off, and popped the trunk.

Pharaoh locked eyes on the pretty little thang coming his way. She reminded him so much of Sasha. The way her long black Raven hair came to a curl at its ends and that golden brown skin tone.

"Hello... I'm Token."

Pharaoh extended his hand, "I'm Pharaoh. "How are you?" he asked walking around to the trunk to get his bags.

"Good. Come on, let me show you the house," said Token. She started back walking toward the front porch.

Pharaoh shook his head at Mo, and smiled. He followed behind Token, getting lost in her. "Thank you," said Pharaoh, as Token held the front door open.

The house was a three-bedroom bungalow; two rooms on the main floor, and one master bedroom upstairs. "This is it," said Token, walking Pharaoh through the house.

All the bedrooms were occupied by either furniture, or Token's shoes and clothes.

"What about the basement?" asked Pharaoh.

"Oh, you want a full tour?"

"Nah, I wanted to know if there was a bed or sofa down there."

"Yeah, there's a pullout, but I won't have you sleeping in no basement. You can sleep in the den. Come on, just let me move all these clothes," Token grabbed two of Pharaoh's bags, then led the way into the den. She set the bags down on the sofa. "This is a pullout, too," she said bending over to pick up the scattered pumps and assorted shoe boxes.

"Can I use your phone?" Pharaoh asked.

"Let's get something straight, you don't have to be asking me for nothing unless you need my help. I know who you are, and what you're doing here. So, relax. My castle is your castle.

"Thank you," said Pharaoh. He picked up the cordless phone off the coffee table and walked into the front room. He called information. "Yes, Sinai-Grace Hospital, please…" The operator put Pharaoh straight through.

"Sinai-Grace, may I help you?"

"Yes, can you tell me if you have a patient by the last name, Dickson…" Pharaoh swallowed hard. He could hear the receptionist typing into the keyboard.

"Yes, we have two actually."

Pharaoh held the phone tight. "We have a Fernando Dickson and a Dorothy Dickson.

Mixed emotions ran through Pharaoh's body. He was happy that his mom, Dorothy was alive, but angered that she must have been shot. "Can you please put me through to Dorothy Dickson's room?"

"I'm afraid, she's still in ICU. She hasn't been assigned to a room yet."

"Can you at least tell me her condition?"

"It doesn't show. It just lists her as being in Intensive Care."

Pharaoh hung up the phone and began pacing the floor.

"Are you okay?" Token asked walking into the front room.

"Does Mo have any guns in the house?" Pharaoh stopped and asked.

"Just two, why?"

"I need one."

"I'll be right back." Token walked toward the back of the house. She came back into the living room carrying a chrome 45. with a black handle. She handed Pharaoh the gun and watched him examine it.

"Yeah, this ought to do it," Pharaoh looked the gun over before tucking it in his waist.

"Mo told me a little bit 'bout what's going on. If you need my help in anyway, I'm yours," said Token.

"Good. Cause I'mma need you to drive me somewhere," said Pharaoh. He walked toward the den where his bags were and stuffed two hands full of money in his pockets, along with his phony driver's license.

"You mean right now?" Token asked following Pharaoh back into the front room.

"Yeah, so put some clothes on. I'll be waiting out in the car."

Token rushed upstairs and snatched the cordless phone off the hook. She pushed speed dial. "Bitch, he is a dime!" yelled Token, as she jumped into a pair of skin tight jeans. "I'm talkin' make yo' pussy wet soon as you see a nigga, fine. Yeah, gotta go. He wants me to drive him somewhere. Call you later. Bye." Click.

Token tossed the phone on the bed before slipping into a new pair of stilettos. She tucked her skin tight wife-beater into her pants, making it stretch to accentuate her nipples. She grabbed her Prada purse and was out the door. Pharaoh sat in the passenger seat of Mo's 420 SL with his seat leaned back and his hoody on his head.

"I hope I wasn't too long," Token said as she climbed behind the wheel, and adjusted her seat.

"Nah, you good," Pharaoh said closing his cell. He had tried calling Ralph one last time.

"So, where to?" Token smiled as she started the car.

Pharaoh gave Token the directions to Sinai-Grace Hospital. She tried making conversation, but all Pharaoh's answers were flat.

"You seem like you've got the weight of the world on your shoulders," said Token.

Pharaoh was looking out the window. He thought to himself. 'That's because I do.'

"Maybe a little music will help," Token turned the radio on low. She sung along to Tina Marie's 'De javu. "Been there before…" Token laughed as she tried to hit the last high-note. She looked over at Pharaoh. 'Poor thing,' she thought. He was lost in his own world…

They pulled into the parking lot of Sinai-Grace. Token asked Pharaoh, "Where you want me to park at?"

"As close to the entrance as you can," said Pharaoh scanning the lot for a decent spot.

Token parked two cars from the entrance and put her hazards on. Pharaoh was writing his mother's name down on a napkin. "Here," he said handing Token the napkin. "I want you to go in and ask what room she's in? Then go up and see if there's any police or anyone else that might look out of place."

"Then what?"

"I'll be down in the lobby. Call my cell and let me know if everything is straight and I'll come up. But if anyone asks, you're a friend of the family."

"Who's Dorothy Dickson?" Token asked reading the napkin.

"It's my mother."

"Oh," Token said softly.

"You ready?" Pharaoh asked, then grabbed the door handle and climbed out the car. He allowed Token to enter the automated sliding door's first and waited a few minutes before stepping inside the lobby. Pharaoh watched from the gift shop as Token walked onto the elevator.

"Can you please ring these up for me?" Pharaoh sat two baskets of flowers and a teddy bear on the counter. He flipped through some get-well-soon cards and put them all on the counter for the young cashier to ring up. "Thank you," said Pharaoh tucking his change and receipt into his pocket. He grabbed the two baskets and a bag off the counter and stepped to the front of the gift shop. His cell phone lit up and vibrated.

"Everything seems normal. There's some family in the room and out in the hall. I'm on the second floor, room 217."

Pharaoh closed his cell shut and took the stairs up to the second floor. He pulled the door open and stepped into the hall. He looked at the room numbers on the wall, and took a left. Pharaoh could see his uncle Toby, his aunt Janice, and his brother Donald all sitting in chairs at the end of the hall. Token met him about half-way down the hall and walked back toward the hospital room with Pharaoh.

"Did you see her?" asked Pharaoh.

"No, I didn't go in," said Token.

Pharaoh's aunt, Janice raised her head at the sound of his voice. She smiled at the sight of Pharaoh. She got up and greeted him with a silent hug. Donald, Pharaoh's brother, awakened. He locked eyes with Pharaoh who was looking at him over Janice's shoulder.

Donald jumped and took a wild swing around their aunt hitting Pharaoh in the side of his face. "You son-of-bitch!" yelled Donald taking another swing. "This is all your fault!"

Their uncle Toby grabbed Donald around the waist and held him back, while he vented.

"It's your fault my momma is laid up in there with tubes running up her nose."

Pharaoh didn't try to fight his brother back. He was right, 'it is my fault,' thought Pharaoh.

Token was standing there in complete shock. She still didn't know what was going on.

"Why don't you go in, and see your mother," said uncle Toby.

Pharaoh took a look at his brother, and tried telling Donald he was sorry with his eyes, as he walked into the room where his mother was. Pharaoh closed the door behind him, and stopped to set the baskets and cards down. His aunt Karen was half asleep in one of the hospital chairs.

"Hi, Pharaoh," she said.

Pharaoh leaned down and gave his aunt a kiss on the cheek. He wiped the sweat from his palms onto his hoody, and pulled the curtain back.

Pharaoh Jr. was holding Ma' Dukes' hand as he slept. Hate and rage filled Pharaoh's soul as he inched toward the bed. He looked at his mother laying there hooked up to all the equipment. Her breathing was heavy, almost as loud as the beeping of the respirator she was hooked up to. Pharaoh brushed his mom's salt and pepper hair from her forehead. "Daddy!" said Jr. He jumped to hug Pharaoh around the waist.

Ma' Dukes' eyes fluttered open while Pharaoh kissed and hugged his son. He picked him up, then turned back to face his mom. Ma' Dukes was smiling from ear to ear at the sight of her baby-boy. "Pharaoh, I knew you'd come," she said, then started coughing.

"Don't try and talk Ma'."

"I'm okay. A couple of bullets ain't gone stop me. I'll be outta here in no time," Assured Ma' Dukes.

"You get your rest, Ma'," Pharaoh sat Jr. down. "Daddy will be out in a little while, let me talk to grandma," said Pharaoh.

"I know what you're going to ask me. Who did this?"

"I know who did it. And I'm going to take care of it," said Pharaoh.

"God is going to take care of him. You just focus on what you need to do so you can get your life back. I don't need you back behind bars."

Pharaoh knew not to argue with Mom' Dukes, so he said nothing. In the back of his mind, he already knew what he was going to do. It was just a matter of when?

"Where'd he shoot you at?" asked Pharaoh.

"In the chest twice; once in the thigh, and once in the back as I tried to reach for my piece. The one that hit me in the back punctured one of my lungs, that's why I'm on this oxygen machine."

Pharaoh couldn't stand to sit there a moment longer. He stood up and gave his mom a kiss. "I'ma see you later. I don't want the feds showing up here on me," he said.

"Baby, please be careful," said Mom' Dukes, holding Pharaoh's hand.

"I will… I love you," Pharaoh kissed her hand, then stepped out of the room.

"Daddy, I want to go with you," said Jr., rushing over to Pharaoh. He clung to Pharaoh's leg.

"Baby-boy, I wish Daddy could take you. But I need you to be a big boy and watch grandma. Can you do that for me?" Pharaoh kneeled down in front of Jr.

"When am I going to see you again?" asked Jr. holding his head down.

'Damn', thought Pharaoh. He didn't want to lie to Jr. "Soon, son," he kissed Jr. on the forehead, and then gave him a hug.

"Go see about grandma."

"Okay…"

Pharaoh rose and said good-bye to his aunts and uncle. He looked at Donald, but thought it be best just to leave…

"Was she alright, what happened?" Token asked as they took the steps down.

"Something that shoulda' never happened?" said Pharaoh. He was talking about Brenda and his mom…

Chapter Three

Lil' One opened the mailbox on her way in from getting her hair done. She pulled the assorted envelopes out the box, and then closed it shut. "Uh, I've been waiting on these," she said looking at the brochures as she walked down the hall to her apartment. She unlocked the door and stepped inside.

"Where you been at, all day?' Tez asked from the sofa. He was rolling two blunts. He had smoked so much of that hydro, that it now took at least two blunts to get him high.

"I told you, I was going to the shop.'

"I don't be listening to you like that. You know I'm high," Tez said imitating Smoky from the movie *Friday*. "What's that you're looking at?" he asked blazing one on the L's.

"Oh, just some brochures from Wayne State University. I'm thinking about going back to school next semester." Lil' One was flipping through the brochures.

"What you taking up, stripper-nomics?" laughed Tez.

"I'd have you to know I graduated from King with a 3.8. Thank you very much." Lil' One was looking over the top of the brochure at Tez.

"Once a good-girl's gone bad, she's gone forever."

"Okay, Jay-Z. What you think, I'ma strip for the rest of my life?"

"What else you gon' do? Now all of a sudden you got aspirations and thangs."

"You're high, so we gon' talk about this later, because you're being offensive."

"Now you wanna use big words and shit. Spell offensive," Tez said taking a pull from his blunt. "Oh, you don't wanna talk now, huh?"

"No, I don't because you're being an ass."

"Nah, I'm being real. You hoes kill me wantin' to go back to school after ya'll realize you done fucked up. Strippin' ain't no steppin' stone. Tell me this, who gon' pay for all this schoolin'?"

"What, you're not going to help me, Tez?"

"I'm not the one having a mid-life crisis. I know who I am. I'm a fuckin' jack-boy, and you's my bitch. You know the basis behind us. We hooked up on some set-up shit. And that's how we gon' keep it."

"I can't even go back to 007 after all that drama."

"There's a hundred clubs you can shake yo' ass in. Trust me you'll find one. So, don't be tryin' to switch up on me."

Lil' One got up from the sofa and stormed to the bedroom. She slammed the door, and then flopped on the bed. She buried her face into the pillows and started crying her eyes out. She couldn't believe that the one person she loved didn't believe in her. Lil' One, would do anything for Tez. But she was starting to see that he wouldn't do the same for her.

"Matter of fact, grab yo' dance clothes. I'ma take you over to All Stars and let them look at you," Tez said standing in the door.

"Get out, Tez!" Lil' One said from the pillow.

Tez walked over to the dresser and stuffed his blunt in the full ashtray. He looked at Lil' One, who was lying on her stomach.

"What did you say?" he asked.

"Get out…" cried Lil' One.

Tez grabbed, Lil' One by her feet, then snatched her to the floor. He reached down and grabbed her under the chin then rag-dolled her. "Bitch, is you stupid," Tez snapped, Lil' One up like four times.

"Stop!" she pleaded.

"Get yo' ass up and go in there and clean yo' self up," Tez said pointing toward the bathroom.

Lil' One held her neck while she walked inside the bathroom.

"And hurry that ass up. I'm tryin' to have you on the stage by midnight," said Tez from the bedroom. He reached in the ashtray and fired his blunt up. "Fuck wrong with that bitch? Ain't no quittin'," said Tez as he blew out a cloud of smoke. He walked in the bathroom. "You ready?"

"Yeah…" said Lil' One. She was looking at the small bruise on her neck in the mirror.

"Let's go." Tez cut the light off, and followed Lil' One into the living room. She grabbed her purse off the sofa, and then snatched the front door open.

"Keep it up and I'ma beat that ass for real," said Tez. He locked the door and fell in step with Lil' One.

Tez kept looking over at Lil' One as he drove down 8 Mile Road. He reached for Lil' One's hand and caressed the back of it, using his thumb. "You needed that," he said.

Lil' One turned from the window and faced Tez.

"Yeah, that's what I said. You needed that. You're getting soft on me. The whole shit with my mom, and now this college shit. That's not the Lil' One I fell in love with. I need you for the long haul," said Tez. He was lying through his teeth. He didn't give a fuck about Lil' One. But his little hot and cold flash was working.

Lil' One started feeling guilty for not being there for Tez. Here it was his mom just got killed and she was making plans to go back to school. "I'm sorry, baby," she said.

Just as Tez knew she would, he used to play that same head game on his baby-mama, Annie, before he wigged out and killed her.

"It's okay. I forgive you," Tez said kissing the back of Lil' Ones' hand. "Let's just not forget our focus," he said.

"Okay," said Lil' One.

Tez pulled into the valet of All Star's strip club on 8 Mile and Hubbel. He and Lil' One got out the car and stepped inside the club.

"My man. Where's Mike?" Tez asked the bouncer.

"Who's asking?"

"Just tell em' it's Tez."

The bouncer picked up the phone and said a few words…

"He'll see you in his office," said the bouncer hanging up the phone.

Tez looked upstairs. Mike was standing in the window with the blinds pulled to the side. He smiled and waved Tez up.

"Come on, baby," Tez and Lil' One walked behind the bar and took the steps up to Mike's office.

"Fuckin', Tez!" Mike said excited from the top of the steps. He hugged Tez and then wrapped his arm around his shoulder. Mike hadn't stopped smiling. He was a middle-aged Arab who owned a lot of Amoco Gas stations around

- 28 -

the city, as well as All Stars. "I thought you were dead or some shit. It's been how long?" asked Mike. He had walked Tez over to his private bar and was fixing him a drink.

"I don't know. But it's been a minute. I see you done up-graded the club with some betta dancers. Them last bitches you had in here had gunshot wounds, c-sections and saggy titties."

"I've got new management... Who's the girl?" asked Mike as he raised his glass to his mouth.

"I want you to meet your new showcase dancer. This is my wife. But her stage name is Lil' One," said Tez.

"Hello," Lil' One said politely.

"She's a looker. But can she dance, I mean really dance?" Mike asked Tez as if Lil' One weren't even standing there.

"Put some music on," Tez told, Mike.

While Mike stepped behind his desk to the stereo player, Tez asked Lil' One to strip down. "Give it to him raw, baby," he said as Lil' One walked Mike by hand over to the leather sofa. She sat him down and then started her number. She turned around and bent over giving Mike a shot of that fresh pussy.

"You see that? New pussy," said Tez. He was kicked back in Mike's desk chair with his feet on the desk. "I want in the business, Mike," he said laughing.

*****

Pharaoh and Token were sitting in the parking lot of 007. "What do you want me to do again, say it one mo' time, so I don't mess it up?" Token asked as she faced Pharaoh.

"I want you to go inside and ask for Chyna, she's a barmaid. Tell her somebody really important to her needs to see her out in the parking lot," said Pharaoh.

"What if she asks who it is?"

"Tell her she has to come out to see, then walk away." Pharaoh didn't want to chance giving Chyna the time to call the police. She was spiteful that way, there was no telling what she might try and do.

Token grabbed the door handle and got out. Pharaoh ducked low with his hoody on, while he watched Token disappear inside the club. Pharaoh clutched the butt of his .45 through the slid pocket on his hoody. He checked the side mirror for any incoming cars, but saw none. A few moments later, Token came walking out of the front door. Chyna was nowhere in sight.

"The bartender says that she's scheduled to work at All Stars tonight. You know they be rotating dancers," Token said starting the car. "You know where it's at?" she asked.

"Yeah, it's on 8 Mile and Hubbel," said Pharaoh.

"Oh, I know where it's at. I was just seeing if you knew. You know, I met Mo' while I was dancing at Pretty Woman. You ever been there?" asked Token.

"A few times, but I didn't really like it."

"Why?"

"It just seemed low-budget."

"You talkin' 'bout the club or the dancers?"

"Both. I didn't like the parking and that one way in, one way out shit. It's a death trap but I'm sure that was before you got there. I might have had a different outlook,"

Pharaoh said, trying to clean it up a little. He could tell Token was taking offense, and that wasn't his intention.

"Thank you," smiled Token. She did a turn around the land strip island on Hubbel. She drove up two blocks and turned into the parking lot of All Stars. She parked next to a platinum Audi sitting on 22's. Pharaoh eyed the car.

"That's sharp, ain't it?" Token said looking over at the Audi.

"Yeah, I like that. Hold on," said Pharaoh as he sat up in his seat. He looked across the parking lot at a woman standing at the trunk of her car. Pharaoh reached for the door handle and got out. Chyna had pulled her barmaid outfit from the trunk and pushed it closed.

"Ahhii!" Chyna jumped back.

Pharaoh had scared the living daylights out of her. He was standing there when she closed the trunk.

"I don't have any money," she said.

Pharaoh pulled his hoody off his head. Chyna put her hands over her face, then slapped Pharaoh hard. "You son of a bitch. Where is my son?" demanded Chyna.

"You mean our son? And you know where he's at. He's with his grandmother."

"Not for long," said Chyna.

"You mean to tell me you're still going to fight this?"

"With every bone in my body," said Chyna. She had been fighting in court to get custody of Jr., after his little incident with the Drano, the court deemed her to be an unfit mother, especially with her occupation.

"I didn't come here to argue," said Pharaoh.

"Good. Well, why are you here?" snapped Chyna.

"Something happened to my mom. Tez shot her."

"Oh my God!" Despite Chyna's dislike for Mom' Dukes, she couldn't help but feel sympathy for her. "This thing is getting outta hand, Pharaoh. Is he going to try and kill me next?"

The thought hadn't crossed Pharaoh's mind, but it was a good possibility. "I don't know, which is why I'm here. I need you to help me find Tez as soon as possible."

"What do you want me to do?" asked Chyna.

"To keep doing what you've been doing. Going to work. I heard he be in 007 on the regular. I need for you to keep your eyes and ears open and to the street. Listen, why don't we go somewhere and talk," Pharaoh said looking at the incoming cars.

"I have to be at work in five minutes," said Chyna looking at her watch.

"Just tell that fool, Mike, you're running late. We won't be but about an hour," said Pharaoh.

"Hold on, let me call inside," Chyna dialed out on her cell.

Pharaoh walked over to the driver's window and Token let the window down.

"Listen, I'ma go with her. I'ma see you back at the house in a few hours," said Pharaoh.

"Hmm. Hm," Token said, then sucked her teeth. She started the car and pulled out the parking space.

"You ready?" asked Pharaoh, walking back over to Chyna's CTS Cadillac.

"Yeah. Where we going?" asked Chyna, as she popped the locks.

"Red Lobster. Your favorite," smiled Pharaoh.

He and Chyna got into the car. She put the car in drive and pulled out the lot.

Chapter Four

Pharaoh and Chyna sat in a booth next to the front window of Red Lobster's. Chyna was staring blankly out the window into the parking lot, while they waited for their food to arrive.

"Chyna, I know our relationship hasn't been what it could be, but I'm asking you to help me for the sake of Jr."

"Please, Pharaoh, don't bring my son into this."

"He is in this. Jr. is the very reason we're both sitting here. Whether we like it or not, we brought him in this world together. And as his parents, we need to do what's best by him."

"And what's that, Pharaoh?"

"Chyna, I never wanted you to lose custody of Jr., I'm not against him being with you, and neither is my mom. Somewhere along the line, you started believing so. I guess because she has custody right now. But that's what is best for Jr., it's better than him being in some home."

Chyna was starting to lighten up. She knew deep down that Pharaoh was telling nothing but the truth.

"You're my son's mother, and I'll do anything to see you happy," Pharaoh said reaching across the table for Chyna's hand. "We've gotta help one another," he said.

"For Jr., and him only," said Chyna.

"That's cool and when this is all over, maybe we can even try and be friends," smiled Pharaoh. "Cause we're not enemies…"

"We'll see," said Chyna. She pulled her head back so the waitress could set their plates down.

"It's been a minute since I had some of this," Pharaoh said biting into a piece of beer battered shrimp. "Damn," moaned Pharaoh. The shrimp was melting in his mouth. He closed his eyes and smiled.

Chyna fought to hold back a smile, but couldn't. It was so hard to stay mad at Pharaoh.

"Is that a smile?" teased Pharaoh.

"No... so, what exactly do you need me to do?" asked Chyna.

"I'm not steppin' foot inside 007, someone may recognize me. Nor am I going to kill that nigga up there. I want you to call me in the event he shows up there. But in the meantime, just keep your ear to the street. Try and find out where he lives."

"That shouldn't be too hard. He's fuckin' this dancer named, Lil' One. I assume that their living together. If not, I can still find out her address."

"See, that's what I'm talking about. A'ight bet. And then she can lead me straight to Tez. When's the next time you'll be at 007?"

"I'm there five nights a week. I was only earning some extra money. I do All Stars every Thursday."

"You know that you don't have to be working so hard, especially at them bars. I wish you'd let me help you. I know you want to go back and get your license."

"I'm saving up right now, so I can get back to school fulltime and have all my bills paid up."

"I tell you what, when this is all over, I'll personally put you through cosmetology school, and put the money behind you to open up a shop."

"You don't have to do that, Pharaoh," Chyna said looking down at her plate.

"I know but I want to."

They finished up their spread of sea foods, drunk some wine and talked mostly about Jr.

"Oh, my God! Pharaoh, we've been in here for almost two hours. I told Mike that I was just running a little late."

"Calm down. Like I said, you won't be working there too much longer. But it is getting late, maybe we should get going," said Pharaoh looking at his phone. He paid the bill and left a nice tip for the waitress.

"Where are you staying?" asked Chyna, as they both shut their doors.

"Oh, with a friend of mine. Somebody the feds don't know about," said Pharaoh.

"I was going to ask you, not that it's none of my business, but whatever happened between you and your wife. What's her name?"

Pharaoh looked out the window. He hadn't thought about Sasha in a long time. Not because he had forgotten about her, but because he still loved her and chose to block her from his mind.

"I'm sorry, Pharaoh."

"Nah, it's okay. Her name is, Sasha. The feds…" Pharaoh was about to tell Chyna the truth about how the feds showed her a picture of Jr., but he knew it would only stir up more bullshit. Chyna would know that he had been denying Jr. in a sense. "The feds turned us all against each other. You know her father is the head of my conspiracy. So, she's upset about Tez telling on him and her brother."

"Did you plan on trying to work things out after you settle things with Tez?"

"I hadn't really thought about it."

"So, who was the girl you were with at the club?"

"My old head's girlfriend."

"You ain't gotta lie to me, Pharaoh. I'm just making conversation."

"I knew you weren't going to believe me. Pull over right here."

"That's a bank, Pharaoh and it's closed. Oh, I get it. You don't want me to know where you're staying," said Chyna.

"It's not like that," said Pharaoh, as Chyna parked in the parking lot of First National Bank on the corner of Kelly Road and 8 Mile.

"It wouldn't be proper for me to show anyone my man's crib. That's all."

"You gon' write your cell number down?" asked Chyna.

"Oh, yeah..." Pharaoh took the ink pen and envelope from Chyna and scribbled his number down. He handed Chyna the envelope and said, "I really enjoyed myself."

Chyna blushed, and then said, "Me too."

"A'ight. You drive safe and remember everything I told you. We're going to turn a new page when this is all over. All of us." Pharaoh grabbed the door handle and climbed out the car. He put his hoody over his head and both hands inside the slid pocket of the sweater. He clutched the handle of the .45 as he cut into the alley-way behind the bank. He looked back to see Chyna's tail lights as she pulled onto 8 Mile.

Pharaoh walked down two blocks to Mo's hide-away. He climbed the three step porch and rung the bell.

"Who is it?" asked Token.

Pharaoh could hear Faith Evans playing in the background, and then the chain unlatching. "It's Pharaoh," he said.

Token looked back at the Princess and smiled. She stood up straight and brushed her clothes, then opened the door. Pharaoh stepped through the door and pulled his hoody off his head. He stopped next to the dining room table as he looked over at the thick red thang sitting on the sofa with her legs bust wide open. Pharaoh's eyes traveled up from her ankle to her gleaming thighs and locked on her camel toe. Pharaoh turned around to face Token. He was about to ask her what ole' girl was doing there, but then he remembered it was her house.

"I want you to meet someone. This is my best friend, Princess."

"Excuse us," Pharaoh said looking at Princess. "Let me holla' at you in the back," he said gently grabbing Token's hand. She raised her eyebrows at Princess, as Pharaoh led her to the den. Pharaoh closed the door behind them.

"What's wrong?" asked Token.

"Nothing, and that's how I want to keep it. I have no say or beef with you having people over to the house because this is your house. But listen, I'm not trying to meet anybody, especially not under my real name."

"I'ma put her out right now," said Token reaching for the door knob.

"Nah, you ain't gotta do that. Just if she or anyone asks, tell em' I'm your cousin from Cleveland or something. You feel me?"

"I got it. You hungry? I cooked some steaks, cabbage, baked potatoes. It's all in the oven."

"I'm good. I'ma take a shower and call it a night. I'll see you in the morning," said Pharaoh.

"Well, good night and holla' if you need me," said Token as she stepped out the room and closed the door and grabbed Princess by the arm. "Come on. It's getting late," she said dragging Princess to the door.

"You 'bout to give him some pussy, ain't you?" whispered Princess.

"He's about to get in the shower so, let's just say that I'll be joining him."

Pharaoh walked out of the den and into the bathroom. He wasn't wearing a shirt.

"Did you see that nigga's chest?" gushed Princess.

"Yes." Token snatched the front door open, before pushing Princess outside and locked the door. Token raced upstairs peeling her clothes off as she climbed the steps. She stopped at her dresser and changed into a matching bra and panty set, then grabbed the cordless phone and called Mo.

"Are you coming over tonight?" she asked.

"Nah, I promised the wife we'd go to the casino tonight. But I'll see you some time tomorrow. Is Pharaoh there?"

"Yeah, but he's in the shower."

"A'ight. Tell him I said I'll check him in the a.m."

"Okay, baby. Talk to you later." Click.

Token tossed the phone on the bed, stepped over to her vanity, sprayed a mist of Prada between her chest, and shook her hair. As she was coming down the steps, Pharaoh was coming out the bathroom. He hadn't seen Token at the top of the steps, he walked toward the den.

Token was mad that she had missed him in the shower. Her pussy was soaked and wet from anticipation. She watched as Pharaoh closed the door to the den. Token sucked her teeth and then went in the kitchen. She grabbed the phone off the wall and walked over to the fridge. "I missed him, girl. Yeah, but tomorrow's a new day."

Chapter Five

Tez had taken his jack-boy mission across town. He had Lil' One dancing five nights a week in All Stars, he convinced Mike through Lil' One's exclusive lap dance to start headlining her. It wasn't about the money. Tez wanted to show Lil' One that she was born to strip. He wanted to go block out any future thoughts of her trying to go back to school and all that other nonsense, as Tez called it. He told Mike he could keep all the headline money, but just to keep pushing Lil' One's name. His only focus was setting niggas up for the kill.

Tez sat in his V.I.P. booth wrapping three blunt papers together. He was stuffing a quarter ounce of DRO' in the blunts. It now took him that much to get high. He was trying his best to smoke all the weed he'd taken from Swift and 'em. He even set a goal to smoke all of it by the end of summer. Lil' One was about to go on stage in about ten minutes, so she slid into the booth to spend some time with Tez.

"Hey, baby," she said kissing Tez on the side of his face.

"Who that bitch-nigga sittin' at the bar with all that sum jewelry on?" Tez asked looking up from his wrap.

Lil' One slightly turned in the direction of the bar. She waited a few seconds, and then looked to see who Tez was talking about. "That's Jesse James. You remember the nigga, Yacht, we got a while ago? That's his man."

"I thought he looked familiar. So, what's up with the nigga, you think he's holding fifty bricks or betta?" Tez asked before sparking his 8 inch L.

"They say he's a millionaire and he got that 600 Coupe out there."

"Yeah, but you know how these nigga's be faking, having their fronts up with only twenty stacks in the stash," Tez said, blowing out the cloud of smoke. He hadn't taken his eyes off Jesse. "But a little practice ain't never hurt nobody. See what's up. Try and set something up," said Tez.

"I got you, baby," Lil' One leaned over and gave Tez a kiss on his cheek, then slid out of the booth.

The DJ saw her climbing the stairs to the stage and gave her a shout-out… "Booty's on duty. All the playas, hustlas, and tricks, I want ya'll to gather round and give it up for my girl Lil' One. Dig deep and don't be cheap. Let's get it, baby!" The DJ spun, Lil' One's theme song. "What yo' life like, cause mine's is real."

Lil' One took to the top of the pole as Benie Siegel ripped the chorus. Every nigga in the club gathered around the stage and paid homage as Lil' One did her number. She slid down off the pole and walked over to the edge of the stage. She broke down into a full split in front of Jesse James. She took his Detroit Tigers fitted hat off him and put it on her head. She rose up from her split and rolled onto her back. Lil' One wrapped her legs around her neck making her pussy push out in Jesse's face. She reached around and spread her pussy lips, while Jesse poured Cristal over her stomach, letting it trickle down the crevasse of her wet pussy.

Niggas went crazy and started tossing bills on the stage, Jesse included. He showered Lil' One with hundred dollars bills, holding them high about his head and letting them sprinkle down on her body. Lil' One did a few more songs, then stepped down off the stage. Jesse James was waiting for her at the bottom step. "What you tryna' choose?" asked Jesse James, as Lil' One stopped in front of him.

"I might," said Lil' One, as she put Jesse's hat back on his head and cocked it the way he had it.

"Let's cut to the chase. I'm tryin' to fuck tonight. What's up? Let's get a room."

"I don't do rooms. See me when you get yo' weight up," Lil' One said, rubbing Jesse's chest as she walked around him.

Jesse for the first time in life was at a loss for words. 'This bitch just bossed up on me,' thought Jesse. He watched Lil' One disappear into the dressing room. He walked over to the bar and paid his tab for the night and took a seat.

"What up, doe? What that bitch on?" Jesse's lil' partna', Blade, asked taking a stool next to Jesse.

"Shit. That bitch don't know who ya' boy is or something. Bitch had the balls to tell me to get my weight up. Don't she know I invented stuntin'?'" said Jesse.

"Shit. I'll give you that one. You was the first to push a six hun'd."

"And the first to push a bitch face down my dick while I'm gettin' blunted. Bitch, I'm Jesse James." Jesse watched, as Lil' One walked out of the dressing room. Jesse sat his bottle on the bar, then tapped Blade on the shoulder as he walked toward Lil' One. He met her in the middle of the bar next to the stage. Lil' One looked up at Jesse, she knew what he was going to say before he said it. Some boss-shit, she figured.

"Bitch, I'ma boss. Him-Him." Jesse said popping his collar. "My weight been up, I ain't out here faking…"

Tez saw the play and slid out his V.I.P. booth and left the club.

"So, where are you taking me, cause I'm not doing no room?" said Lil' One.

"I'ma take you to paradise. Show you how a real nigga do," Jesse led the way out the club. He had nodded and gave dap to all his niggas on the way out. The valet driver pulled Jesse's midnight blue 600 Coupe up to the door. He walked around and jumped in the car. Lil' One pretended to be digging in her purse, but she was scanning the lot for Tez.

He sat up in his seat so that Lil' One could see him. Relieved, Lil' One climbed in the passenger seat. As soon as she closed the door, Jesse skirted out the lot. He turned up the volume to his local rap hit he'd put out through a label he started. "Street-lordz, we comin' to yo' city, man…" went the chorus. Jesse snapped in straight boss-mode. He and all his niggas had this thing where it was illegal for a bitch to get in their car and not give them some head. Jesse pulled his pants down and slid out of his boxers. He reached for the back of Lil' One's head and pushed her face down on his dead dick.

While Lil' One skulled him up, Jesse dug into the ashtray and pulled a half-smoked blunt out. He put it in his mouth, then pushed the cigarette lighter in. He set fire to the blunt and stuck the lighter back in its hole. He took a long pull from the L and laid back his seat gripping the wheel with one hand stretched out.

Lil' One was serving him good. She held the base of his dick gently and rubbed the head against the insides of her jaw. Jesse looked down at Lil' One's face, but her eyes were closed. Whether if it was the weed, or just plain déjà vu, Jesse started to recall where he knew Lil' One from. The night he was over on the eastside with Yacht at 007 flashed through his mind. He looked up at the road, then back down at Lil' One. He remembered Yacht leaving the club with her that night, and that was the last time he seen Yacht alive. Jesse veered off the road. He had been traveling down the shoulder of the Southfield expressway. He made a right on 9 Mile Road and checked his rear-view. He made another sudden right on Greenfield, while still playing his mirrors. He focused in on the headlights as they bent the corner. It was the same car that had been making every turn with him. Jesse pulled, Lil' One up from his dick. "That's enough," he said fixing his clothes.

"Lil' One saw the intersection of 8 Mile approaching. "Why are you going back toward the city?" she asked.

"I forgot something at the club. Just relax. I'ma blow yo' back out in a little while," said Jesse, as he made the turn onto 8 Mile.

Lil' One dug in her purse and answered her cell. "What's up girl?" she said speaking into the side mirror.

"Listen, to me baby. I think that nigga seen me following him. I can tell by the way he's switching lanes and making all these turns…" said Tez.

"Nah, I got an appointment to get my hair and nails done tomorrow. I'll see you at the club," said Lil' One.

When he makes his next turn, blow his shit loose," Tez hung up.

"Okay. Talk to you later." Click.

Lil' One dug inside her purse as if she were just putting her cell away. But she came out her purse with her .380 and pointed at the side of Jesse's temple. Boom! Boom! She blew his brains all over the driver's window. The car rolled and hit the curb in between the land island where they sat waiting on traffic to slow down.

Lil' One calmly brushed her prints from the car, then climbed out. She walked around the front of the car and got in the Audi. Tez pulled onto 8 Mile and checked his side mirror to make sure he wasn't being followed. Jesse was slumped over leaning against the driver's door.

"I told you he was just practice," said Tez.

Chapter Six

"My nigga, what you done did to this bitch? She ain't been lookin' out to bring me my packages. I'm startin' to lose weight," said Ollie.

"Man, sit tight. I'ma holla' at her and make sure you're straight," Pharaoh was stretched across the sofa in the den. Ollie's call had awakened him.

"And what's this shit she's tellin' me about you being back in Detroit. Is you know who outta there?"

"Nah, not yet, but I'm working on it."

"Man, I did what you said and had my lawyer file for a speedy-trial. Dawg, don't leave me stranded come trial day. I don't want no surprises," said Ollie.

"I'ma get it done. Matter of fact, I'm gettin' up now."

Beep. Beep. "You hear that? That's my phone, the battery is almost dead, and ole' girl actin' like she ain't tryna charge me up."

"Just chill, I'ma holla' at her, my nigga. And I'ma give her some bread to give you."

"A'ight. I'ma holla' back." Ollie's phone went dead.

Pharaoh looked at the time on his phone. It was 9:30 a.m. He rolled off the sofa and went inside the bathroom. He used the toilet, then brushed his teeth and washed his face. As he was coming out the bathroom, the smell of bacon and scrambled eggs hit him in the face. He followed the aroma into the kitchen and stopped in the door. Token was at the stove doing the mothafucka. She had three skillets burning; one with eggs, one with bacon, and another with pancakes.   To top it all off she was standing there in nothing but her house shoes, wife-beater and a thong. She turned around and smiled. "Good morning," she said.

"Who you cookin' all this food for?"

"You and me. And maybe, Maurice. He sometimes stops by before going to the shop. Have a seat, and let me fix you a plate."

Token handed Pharaoh the remote control to the small plasma mounted on the wall next to kitchen table. He took a seat and turned on the TV. He flicked to the Channel 4 News.

"They've been showing that story all morning," said Token as she turned from the stove.

Pharaoh put a little volume on the News. "That's Jesse James," Pharaoh said, as Jesse's mug-shot flashed across the screen. The camera flashed to a wide shot of All Stars. The anchor explained that Jesse was last seen alive at the club.

"That's fucked up," said Token.

"Yeah… but that's the game," Pharaoh turned from the TV and Token's titties were right there. They were centimeters from Pharaoh's lips. Token leaned over Pharaoh giving him a full view as she set his plates down in front of him. She turned on her heels and slung that ass as she walked back over to the stove.

"You comfortable?" Pharaoh asked, then started laughing.

"Yeah.. What you trippin' off my thong?" Token asked looking down at her thighs. It gets too hot in here when I'm cookin'. What you never had a woman cook you breakfast in a thong?"

"Yeah, my woman."

"What you mean by that?" Token sat her plates down and took a seat across from Pharaoh.

"Just so we're clear. Mo's my man, and I would never disrespect…"

"What are you talking about?" Token bit into a slice of bacon and chewed seductively.

"Let's be real, we're both grown. I see how you keep throwin' yo' ass around. But let me tell you somethin', I'm used to having bad bitches, so that shit doesn't move me…"

"You ain't never had a bitch as bad as me," Token said admitting her intentions.

"I'ma let you believe that, so long as we keep it respectful."

"Maurice ain't got to know."

"Yeah, but I'll know. And that's not me," Pharaoh said standing. "Thank you for the breakfast," he said then walked out the kitchen.

Token got up and followed him into the den. His loyalty to Mo' only made her want him more. "I can respect that you know," she said as Pharaoh slid into a pair of jeans. "You being loyal to Maurice and all… I guess all men aren't alike."

"Nah, don't get me wrong. I gets mine! But just not with my people's people."

"That's just it. I'm tired of being just Mo's side-chick. I figured you were single…"

"Token, I'm not 'bout to discuss my man's business behind his back, but I will share some of my experience with you. Just because your Mo's mistress or whatever, doesn't mean that he doesn't love you. It's hard to explain, but trust me.

Men are capable of really loving more than one woman. And I'm sure Mo' loves you."

"Thank you. I needed to hear that. So, are we still cool?" she asked, as Pharaoh slid his hoody on.

"Fo' sho'." Pharaoh shot Token a smile, and then picked up his cell phone.

"You need me to take you somewhere?" she asked.

"Nah, I'ma just bend a few corners and check some things out. Maybe we can do lunch or something, seeing as though I spoiled breakfast."

"No, that was my fault. But I'd like that." Token, followed Pharaoh out into the living room and let him out.

Maurice was pulling up as Pharaoh walked down the steps. Mo hit his horn, then got out.

"Boy, where you going this early? You ain't got no job?" laughed Mo as he extended his hand pulling Pharaoh in for a hug.

"I'm just getting' out and seein' what's what."

"I brought you something." Mo said handing Pharaoh the keys to a black 500 SL Benz with tinted windows. "It's a step down from what you're used to pushin', but uh,…"

"Nah, it's good!" Pharaoh said excited.

"Yeah, I got it from Exotic Cars. It's paid up for six months. So, now you can cruise the city behind tint."

"How much I owe you?" asked Pharaoh.

"Ahh… Don't worry about it. You just take care of your other business. You know Brenda's wake is this morning. Tez will more than likely be there, but I don't want you involving his moms. Let's her go out in peace," said Mo.

"I wouldn't waste my time. Knowing Tez, he probably won't even show."

"Yeah, you're right," laughed Mo.

"I'ma get out of here. But thanks again, man, I really do appreciate you."

"Shit, who knows, I may need your help one day. What she in there doing?"

"Oh, cookin' breakfast. You oughta' get in there before it gets cold," said Pharaoh. He hit the unlock button on the key chain and the Benz's lights flashed.

Pharaoh sunk into the deep plush tan leather seat and just sat there for a moment. He ran his hands across the steering wheel and the wood-grain on the dash. It brought back memories of him, Tez and Ollie hopping out 600's. Pharaoh's cell phone vibrated on his hip breaking his trance. "Who this?" he cautiously answered not recognizing the number.

"What, it's been that long?" You don't remember my number?" asked Chyna.

"It has been a minute. What's up, where you at?" asked Pharaoh. He stuck the key in the ignition and started the car.

"At work."

"You stay at work. Do you need some money?"

"Nah, I'm cool, but thank you. I've got some information for you. You got a pen?"

Pharaoh scanned the car before leaning over. "Hold on, let me see," he said digging through the glove box. "Go ahead, what is it?" Pharaoh closed the glove box and sat up with his pen and paper ready.

"It's 2300 Schaefer," said Chyna.

"And what's this to?"

"It's the address listed on that little bitch's application. Her real name is Tameka Hanson.

"I got it," said Pharaoh.

"I suppose you're going to check it out, so be careful and call me later."

"I'ma do that. And good – lookin' out." Pharaoh closed his cell and sat up in his seat. He was familiar with Schaefer. It was two blocks from where his great uncle Snookie lived. Pharaoh opened the Benz up as he breezed down the ramp onto the Davidson expressway. Within minutes, he was coming up on Dexter. He made a left cutting through the CitGo gas station and back onto Dexter.

Pharaoh held the piece of paper with the address up to his face "2300" he said, a he turned down Schaefer. He had just realized that Schaefer was an industrial street. There were no houses, but he kept on in pursuit of 2300. He looked at the address painted on the 48 Cleaners and knew his address had to be next. He pulled over at the curb and parked.

Pharaoh leaned over the console and squinted inside the automotive shop. The garage door was up, but Pharaoh saw no one. He secured his .45 in his waist, then reached for the door handle. Pharaoh walked around the front of the car and as he was climbing the curb, an old man maybe in his sixties stepped out of the garage. He was wearing an oiled covered blue Dickie's overall jumpsuit and was wiping gook from his hands onto a rag.

"I don't fix on foreign cars," the old man said of Pharaoh's Benz.

Pharaoh hadn't missed a step despite the old man's information. "I was hoping you could tell me where I can find Tameka Hanson." Pharaoh read from the paper, then looked back up at the old man.

"What do you want with my Princess? She owes you something?" The old man frowned his face.

"I wouldn't say owe, but I really need to find her."

The old man turned and started walking through the garage. "You can come in, I'm just going to fix myself some coffee."

Pharaoh followed behind the old man, stopping at a steel folding tray stand where the aged coffee maker sat. "Can you tell me where to find her?"

"I haven't seen Tameka in I don't know how long. She used to live upstairs in the apartment. I came to work one day and she had taken most of her things. I don't know what's wrong with that girl," the old man said, staring at the floor.

"Do you at least have her cell number?"

"Yeah, but I'm not gone waste my breath calling her. She knows where I'm at." The old man raised his Styrofoam cup to his mouth and slurped at the hot coffee. As he lowered the cup, Pharaoh had his 45 drawn and pointed at his gut.

"You're going to pick up that phone old man, and get Tameka on the line," whispered Pharaoh.

"Nigga, fuck you. I'm not doing a mothafuckin' thing. What you gone do, shoot me?" the old man nonchalantly raised his cup halfway to his mouth, then threw the scalding hot coffee in Pharaoh's direction.

"Ahh... shit," said Pharaoh. Nursing his neck where the coffee struck him. He gave chase up the flight of stairs behind the old man. He tackled him around the ankles as they reached the top stair. Pharaoh climbed on top of the old man and put his pistol to his mouth.

"You old fucker. I'ma tell you one last time to pick up the phone and call Tameka, or I'ma..."

The old man spit a luggie between Pharaoh's eyes. "I'm not callin' nobody. You young punk!"

Pharaoh stood up and pointed his gun down at the old man's forehead. Boom! One shot put him to rest. Pharaoh looked at the crater sized hole in the man's forehead. Brain matter was everywhere.

Pharaoh scrambled around the apartment. It was pretty much empty, except for the furniture. He pushed the door open to one of the bedrooms, he could tell that the room once belonged to a woman by the flower patterned blanket and the sweet scent of perfume lingering in the air. Pharaoh walked over to the dresser and picked up the lone picture frame. It was a picture of the old man and Lil' One, when she was a little girl. Pharaoh looked at the picture closer, and removed it from its frame. He tucked the picture in his back pocket then left.

Chapter Seven

"It's been two days, and you still haven't seen either one of them?" asked Pharaoh.

"Nope. They haven't been in here. I thought you took care of them or something," said Chyna. She was talking on the phone mounted on the wall behind the bar inside 007.

"Nah, that information you gave me was to her father's automotive shop."

"Well, that's what she had on her application as her home address. You know don't nobody really check on that stuff."

Pharaoh had turned down Syracuse Street. "Yeah. Well, uh just keep yo' eyes and ears open for me. That nigga bound to show up."

"Okay, talk to you later," said Chyna. Click.

Pharaoh smiled to himself at the sight of ole' Tony Rome coming out the gas station. He was tailing some white man shooting his shot. 'Probably tryna' talk him outta something,' thought Pharaoh. He continued up the block. He crossed Hillsdale Street and brought the Benz to a slow creep. There was a dice game in full swing on the basketball court in the park. Pharaoh became furious. He looked at all the niggas from his hood; John John, Damond, Ronnie D., Lemon Head and Pope. They were all crunched in a circle shooting dice. "Bitch-ass niggas," Pharaoh said looking in the rear-view at them. He was angry because when word hit the street that Tez was snitching, not one of them stepped up to the plate and handled the nigga. They were so much afraid of Tez, that they let him remain in the hood. Them niggas couldn't be on the block no more, Pharaoh told himself. He clutched the handle of his .45 and was getting ready to park at the end of the block, but two white agents were parked on the corner facing Tez's house. Pharaoh drove pass the blue Lumina and stared the passenger dead in his face.

The agent couldn't see Pharaoh's face because of the tinted windows. Pharaoh looked down and turned the radio on. "I live the life of a thug nigga, until the day I die," Pharaoh sung along to Pac's 'All eyes on me.' He sat up in his seat and looked in the rear-view mirror. The blue Lumina had gotten behind him. Pharaoh's stomach did a flip. He took a deep breath as he turned onto Nevada. The Lumina turned with him. Pharaoh drove about four streets over and made a right. The Lumina made a right behind him.

"Fuck!" said Pharaoh. He made his mind up. If they made this next turn with him, he was going to open the Benz up. He reached the corner of Fenlon and Hillsdale and made another right. The agents hadn't even stopped they hugged the corner right behind Pharaoh.

Pharaoh figured they might not be waiting on back up or something, that's why they hadn't flicked their lights. But Pharaoh wasn't about to wait for back up to arrive. He punched the gas down and the Benz shot off like a rocket. Looking in his rear-view, Pharaoh could see the dash strobe light inside the Lumina come on, as well as the headlights. The chase was on.

"Cause all I do is floss my shit. Five-doube O…" what better music than Pac while on a high-speed chase? Pharaoh had the agents by a blocks difference. He was coming up on the intersection of Mound Road, but he hadn't planned on slowing down or stopping. Pharaoh saw his opening on both sides of the busy traffic. He floored the 500 straight across Mound; cars were slamming on the brakes and honking their horns. He looked in the rear-view as he made it across. The agents had tried the same cross move, but as they crossed the second side a pickup truck creamed the ass of the Lumina making it spin out.

Pharaoh turned the corner of St. Louis before he could see what else took place. His heart was racing as he continued to gun the Benz down to Six Mile Road then made a turn heading into Hamtramck, Michigan. The only thing Pharaoh could think about was his mom, Jr., and the promise he made Ollie. He couldn't go to jail now, he thought, while constantly checking his mirrors. He turned onto the Chrysler freeway and took it back to Kelly Road. He started to relax as he made the turn around and pulled in front of Mo's house. He put the car in park and cut it off. He got out and walked around the back of the car. Pharaoh realized that the agents couldn't trace the Benz because all he had was a temp tag in the window.

'I'm still gone have to park it until Mo gets my plates,' he thought walking up the side walk and climbing the three step porch.

Token swung the door open and Pharaoh stepped in. He took a seat on the sofa.

"What's wrong, you look like you just seen a ghost?" asked Token taking a seat next to Pharaoh.

"I almost blew it," said Pharaoh.

"What happened?"

"I almost let the feds catch me. They just chased me through my old neighborhood. All while they were chasing me, the only thing I could think about was. I can't go back to jail. Not right now," Pharaoh said flashing back to the chase.

"Well, if you need me to drive you somewhere, I can." Token said softly.

"I appreciate it." Pharaoh stared blankly at the wall. He knew that he'd just escaped by the luck of the draw. 'I gotta hurry up and catch this nigga,' he thought of Tez.

Chapter Eight

Tez had Lil' One so busy dancing and setting niggas up, she didn't even know her father was killed. Tez had been scheming on this fat red old nigga named Amp. Amp had been playin' All Stars the past few days. His homecoming party was held there and the nigga just sorta never left. After spending seven years in the feds for conspiracy, all Amp wanted to do was suck on them young girls' pussies. His paper was said to be long from his run in the game, and so far his legend proved to be true.

Tez watched from his V.I.P. booth as Amp made it rain. The old freak nigga had two shoe boxes full of money sitting in front of him and was passing it out to the strippers like it was toilet paper. That's what he called anything less than a hundred, toilet paper.

"Ya'll bitches might as well take this lil' shit, I ain't gone do nothin' but wipe my ass with it," laughed Amp.

His cohort, Harold, joined him in laughter .

"I tell ya'll what, if ya'll wanna make some real money, let's all go back to my place when the club closes." Amp was looking Lil' One dead in her eyes as she grinded against his limp dick.

"Sounds good to me," Lil' One whispered, in Amp's ear. She had his old ass all geeked up and ready to spend a fortune.

The club was about to close in ten minutes, and all the ballas were selecting which chicks they wanted to take to the room. Amp had five strippers, Lil' One included.

"I'll be right back. Just let me get dressed."

Amp gripped his crotch as he watched Lil' One to the dressing room. "That's a bad little bitch," Amp said, turning to finish his drink.

"Who you tellin'," ole' Harold added.

"I'ma round up the rest of these hookers, pay the tab and let lil' moma know we outside in the limo." Amp grabbed his shoe boxes, opened the lids and tossed the remainder of the bills over his head. He laughed as niggas and dancers scrambled to the floor in pursuit of that green. He grabbed up the chicks he had told was leaving with him and stepped out the club.

Tez slid out his booth and into the dressing room. "What are you doin' in here?" One stripper asked, while trying to cover her breast.

Tez stopped and looked the chick up and down. "Bitch, you just got finished showin' yo' titties and the crack of yo' ass. Stop faking." He walked over to the locker where Lil' One kneeled stuffing her thong and heels inside her suitcase.

"What that old fool talkin' 'bout?" Tez whispered.

"He's taking 'bout five of us back to his place. Wherever that is…" Lil' One closed her case and stood up.

"This what I want you do to. When ya'll get out there. Call me and give me the address and directions. I got a little surprise for ole' fat ass."

Lil' One, gave Tez a kiss on the cheek. "See you in a minute." She lifted the handle of her suitcase and rolled it out the dressing room.

"Can you leave now?"

Tez looked at the chick and bald his face up. "Bitch, shut the fuck up. You tack head slut..." Tez pushed the door open and walked to the front door. As he was waiting on the valet to pull his car around, Tez could see Amp's fat funky ass in the back of a stretch Lincoln limo. He was sniffing powder from in between one of the stripper's chest. 'Yeah get high you fat fuck'. Tez thought, as the limo pulled away.

"We got a long drive to the house. What ya'll gone do, ya'll gone put on a show for me?" asked Amp. He already had his pants unfastened.

"What you want us to do?" asked Lil' One, as she spread her legs wide open and jacked her mini skirt high on her thighs. She wasn't wearing any panties.

"You," Amp said to the stripper seated next to him. "Eat her pussy," he ordered.

Lil' One rolled her skirt up to her waist and raised her legs, cocking them wide for the chiny-eyed girl. The girl got on her knees and began lapping her tongue across Lil' One's pussy.

"Hmmm," Lil' One moaned, while palming baby girl's head.

Amp crawled behind the girl who was heading Lil' One up, and pulled down her jeans. He slid his limp dick down the crack of her ass into her warm wet pussy. Amp sunk into the girl's juices and closed his eyes. He began stroking her from the back making her soft ass cheeks slap hard against his pelvis.

Ole' Harold was on the bench seat getting head by the other three chicks. They were all on their knees sharing

Harold's cum as he bust off. The driver pulled into Amp's private estate in Monroe, Michigan. He pulled around the circular driveway up to the front door and parked. Amp and Harold were both sweatin' bullets and the back of the limo had a foul stench going, whether it came from them or the strippers, it was undecided. Amp pulled his slacks up and wiped his forehead of the sweat.

"Leave the sunroof cracked," he said climbing out the limo.

Ole' Amp had long old money. Porsches, Jaguars and custom Lacs surrounded the estate. He led the strippers through the large wooden double door inside the mansion. The strippers were all wowed, just as Amp expected.

"Harold, give em' a tour of the house, then ya'll go and get ready. I'ma take a quick shower." Amp directed the festivities. He climbed the oak staircase, while Harold showed the girls the house.

Lil' One fell back and called Tez. "Yeah, we're in the Swan Village estates in Monroe, Michigan. The address is 18541 Alexander   Blvd."

"I'm on my way. Unlock the door for me." Click.

        Lil' One crept back to the front door and unlocked it. She took the staircase up where she had seen Amp go. She walked down the long hallway looking in each room, all of which were empty. At the end of the hall was Amp's master bedroom. Lil' One pushed the door open and stepped inside. She could hear Amp singing in the shower, and then the water turned off. She lay across the bed in a sexy position, and waited for Amp to come out the bathroom.

"I know that I'm living... For the love of you... Yeah..." Amp sung his version of the Isley Brothers tune, as he stepped out the bathroom into the bedroom. He hadn't seen Lil' One sprawled across the bed, ass cocked. Amp was wiping his face with his towel. He stepped over to his dresser and pulled out a fresh pair of drawers.

"There's no need for those tonight."

Amp turned around to see Lil' One playing with her pussy. She motioned for him come here with her finger. Amp let his towel drop to the floor and crawled up the bottom of the bed on all fours. He lay beside Lil' One and spread her thighs. He stuck his finger in her pussy and then sucked the juice from his finger. "This lil' pussy tastes like a peach."

Lil' One rolled Amp onto his flabby back and climbed onto his stomach. She leaned down and began sucking on his neck while jacking his dick. "Let me tie you up," Lil' One whispered in Amp's ear. He was so lost in the moment that he agreed.

"Go ahead."

Lil' One rolled off Amp and dug through his dresser drawers. She couldn't find anything that she could use. She turned toward the closet and grabbed five neck ties. "I'm 'bouts to fuck your brains out," said Lil' One smiling. She mounted Amp's chest and began tying his wrist to the poles of the headboard.

"That's right. Make em' extra tight, baby." Amp smiled and closed his eyes, as Lil' One tied his ankles to the pillars. She climbed back on top of Amp and wrapped the last tie around his mouth. She tied it tight, then kissed the side of his face. Amp's eyes bucked as he realized what was going on.

"Hmm… You sit tight." Laughed Lil' One. "Get it, sit tight?" she laughed on her way out the room.

"Where's Amp?" Harold asked from the sectional sofa in the living room. He was seated between two of the girls.

"Oh, he'll be down in a minute. He had to take another shower." Lil' One positioned herself on the sectional where she could see the door. All the other girls were treating their noses and taking turns sucking Harold's dick. Lil' One dug in her purse and gripped the handle of her 380 as she saw Tez creep through the front door. He silently shut the door, then made eye contact with Lil' One. She nodded toward the living room, then come out her purse. Boom! Lil' One blew the chicks brains out who had been sucking Harold's dick. Boom! Boom! She dropped the other girl dead in her tracks.

Boom! Boom! Boom! Tez set fire to Harold's nappy chest. His body jerked violently, and a fourth shot put him to rest. Boom! Tez planted a slug dead center of Harold's forehead sending his brains flying out the back of his head.

Lil' One gave chase to the other two strippers and shot them both in the back of the head.

"Where's fat boy?" asked Tez, as Lil' One walked back into the living room.

"He's tied up." Lil' One led the way up the oak staircase.

Tez pulled the tie out of Amp's mouth.

"You know who I am, huh?" shouted Amp.

Tez sat on the edge of the bed and rubbed Amp's forehead with the barrel of his .40 cal.

"Of course, you're the man who's going to make me a millionaire tonight."

"You funky bitch. You set me up," Amp snared at Lil' One.

"Shh… Look at me Amp. I'm talking to you," said Tez.

"What do you want?" Amp was sweatin' bullets.

"Where's the money? And I'm only going to ask you once, or you can join Harold in hell." Tez pressed his gun to the side of Amp's head and gripped his fat chin.

"Downstairs in the basement underneath the bar."

Tez nodded to Lil' One and she cut out.

"You betta not be lying to me, Ampy boy."

"You're not going to kill me, are you?" Amp's eyes were filled with fear.

"Of course, but I'll make it quick and painless. But if you're lying… well, just hope you're not lying." Tez continued to rub his pistol across Amp's face. He wiped the tears from his face with the barrel. "Don't cry, Amp. It's not that bad…"

Lil' One raced back into the room. She was out of breath and breathing heavy.

"Was it down there?" Tez looked up from Amp.

Lil' One nodded yes. "A lot," she gasped.

Tez rose to his feet and pressed his barrel into Amp's dome. "Close your eyes, Amp. When you wake up you'll be dead." Tez, waited for Amp to close his eyes, and then blew his skull loose. Boom!

Tez and Lil' One stuffed all the stacks of old money into Hefty trash bags, three in total. Tez dug around the secret compartment under the bar for anything else.

"That's everything, baby," said Lil' One.

"That fat bastard gave it up too easy. He's got some more money put up somewhere." Tez stood up and put his hands on his hips, while he looked around the basement.

"This is enough. Tez, we need to get going."

Tez looked at the three trash bags and said, "Yeah, you're right." He threw two bags over his shoulder and led the way upstairs.

"How much you think's in there?" asked Lil' One, as Tez put the bags in the trunk of his Audi.

"We can count it after we roll around naked in it."

Chapter Nine

"Why don't you just put a ticket on his head? You know these thirsty niggas out here will turn his ass in," said Chyna.

"I tried that, but believe it or not, ain't none of these niggas tryin' to see Tez. They scared of him." Pharaoh was leaned against Chyna's CTS with his hoody over his head. They were in the parking lot of Auto Zone around the corner from 007.

"This is the longest I've seen him go without coming through the club. Maybe he's dead," suggested Chyna. She folded her arms and surveyed the traffic behind Pharaoh's back.

"I doubt it seriously. And if he is, I'ma digh is ass up to make sure. Look, just keep doing what you've been doing, and he'll turn up."

"I went to see your mom yesterday."

Pharaoh looked at Chyna and raised his eyebrows,

"I thought about what you said, and you were right. She's not the one keeping me from Jr."

"How was she?" Pharaoh asked with his head down.

"Better. She's still on the respirator, but he's sitting up and alert."

:Jr.?"

"Spoiled rotten… I can't wait to bring him home, and for things to go back to normal."

"I know. Me, too. Look, I'ma get going. You keep me informed." Pharaoh gave Chyna a hug, then brushed her hair to the side of her face.

Chyna broke their stare. "Yeah, I gotta get to work myself. I'll call you later," she said, sliding out of Pharaoh's arms and into her car.

Pharaoh took a deep breath, and then turned around. He climbed in the passenger seat of Token's Explorer and closed his eyes.

"She's pretty. Who is that, your girlfriend?" Token asked, backing out from her parking space.

"My son's mother."

"Oh… Ya'll not together?"

"We never were. Our son is something that just happened. But we're trying to work thing out as far as being cordial for the sake of our son."

"Pharaoh, can I ask you a question?" Token turned in her seat.

"Sure."

"What's really going on with you? I mean, every time I look at you, it's as if you're a million miles away. Lost in your own world. Mo told me who you were, and that you're on the run, but from what?"

"My past," sighed Pharaoh. "It's haunting me…"

"Is it something that can be fixed?"

"That's what I've been working on." Pharaoh paused, before continuing. "My best friend is out to ruin my life. Someone who I once loved, and for some reason, I still got love for him. He has destroyed my life completely. The only way I can get my life back is to take his."

"There has to be another way, Pharaoh."

"I wish there was," Pharaoh said looking out the window at two little boys crossing the street in front of the Explorer. They reminded him of Tez and himself, back in the day, before the money, envy and betrayal. Back when they were just friends. The light turned green and token drove on.

"Well, I hope you get your life back..." Token said, before turning the radio on low.

'Me too,' thought Pharaoh. 'Me too.'

Chapter Ten

Lil' One and Tez stayed up all night counting the money they had taken from Amp. It came out to $1,450,000; the most money either of them had ever possessed in their entire lives. Tez wasted some of the money on frivolous things like fur, some mink drawers and a purple scarf which he wore tied around his head like Jimmy Hendrix. Tez was walking around the apartment chain smoking blunts. He'd hit them twice, put it out, and spark another one. He did this while doing a constant recount of the money.

"You got change for a hun'd?" Tez asked Lil' One, peeling a hundred dollar bill off the stack he held in his hand.

"Let me see. Nope, all I got is hun'ds," laughed Lil' One. She was sprawled across the bed laying on nothing but hundred dollar bills. "What we gone do with all this money?" she asked Tez.

Tez spun around from pouring himself a drink. He looked at Lil' One and said,

"Spend it," then downed his glass of Henny.

"Don't you think we should invest some of it?"

"Here you go again with this, I have a dream shit. I told you, I'ma jack-boy. And you's my bitch. So, play yo' role..." Tez poured himself another drink and tossed it back... He climbed on the bed next to Lil' One. "We gon' do this shit until the end of time. We gone be 80 years old still robbing muthafucka's," laughed Tez.

Lil' One faked a smile. She knew that Tez was dead serious. And that they'd be broke in no time looking for their next victim.

"What time you going to work? We gotta keep you in the midst of thangs."

"I was going to take the day off and go do some shopping. You know I've gotta stay lookin' good for you and them suckas, baby." Lil' One was playing on Tez intelligence, so he'd let her take the day off.

"You can do some shopping, but you still need to have that ass on the stage tonight. I'ma go look at some cars." Tez rolled off the bed and fired up another blunt.

Lil' One laughed. "I hope you're not going lookin' like that. You look like Rick James," she laughed.

"Oh, so you get it. That's my nigga," Tez said looking down at his get-up. "I think I am going like this," he said leaving out the room.

Lil' One started stuffing bills into her Prada purse while constantly looking down the hall. She wasn't about to sit back and allow Tez to blow all their money. She was going to make some investments. 'He won't miss it. He'll blow, through it and won't even know this is missing.' Lil' One told herself while filling her purse to the max. She rushed inside the bathroom, grabbing her clothes along the way. She dressed and fixed her hair in the mirror, then walked out into the living room. She looked around and Tez was already gone. 'Good,' she thought.

Lil' One grabbed her car keys and was out the door. She jumped in her Dodge Shadow and turned the key. The car turned over, jerked then shut off. The engine made a hissing sound. It had been a while since she last drove the car. Lil' One turned the key once more and gave it some gas. She looked in the rear-view mirror at the thick cloud of white smoke coming from the tail-pipe, then at the oil light flashing on the dashboard. She added an oil change to her list of things to do, as she backed out and pulled out the complex.

*****

"Bitch, I'm pulling up now. So, come out." Lil' One closed her cell phone and honked her horn twice. She saw the curtain to the house brush back, and then the front door swung open.

"Girl, where we going?" her friend asked climbing into the passenger seat.

"Shopping."

"You need to be shoppin' for a new car. You mean to tell me, all that money you say yo' man is getting' and he ain't put you in no new car?"

"Never mind my love-life." Lil' One pulled away from the curb and crossed the turnaround leading into the Eastland Mall parking lot on Kelly Road. "Did you get the dick?" she asked her friend.

"I'm working on it. He's playin' hard to get."

"I got something I need you to hold," Lil' One said reaching under her seat.

"What is it?"

"Here." Lil' One handed her friend the Prada purse.

"Girl... Where'd you get all this money?"

"I said for you to hold it, not spend it. You remember when we first started dancin' we said that we'd do it until we

could save up enough money to open up our own salon. Well, somewhere along the way we both got side tracked. You found a sponsor and I've been chasin' up behind my crazy ass boyfriend." Lil' One had the nerve to valet park her smoking Shadow. She continued speaking as they walked through the mall's entrance. "That money is for the shop. And I'ma bring you some more."
They cut into Marshal Field's Department store and walked over to the Dolce & Gabbana section.
"What about our license. We gotta go back to school."
"I'ma take some business classes at Wayne State in the morning. I need you to enroll in Cosmetology school. I can work under your license until I can go back."
"You've been thinking about this for a while, huh?"
Lil' One looked at her friend. "Yeah, cause this nigga I'm with, he's bound to go to jail or wind up dead. I gotta start thinking for me."
        They dug through the racks and tore Dolce & Gabbana up, along with a few other designers. After shopping, they hit the food-court and grabbed a slice of pizza. They continued to detail their plans on how they'd both get from under their boyfriends dependency. Lil' One looked at her watch and it was going on 5:00. She wanted to stop and get a quick oil change before she went to work. She dropped her friend off at home, and then stopped by the Jiffy-Lube on the corner of 8 Mile and Sherwood.
                    *****
"I'm on my way to work. They got me working at All Stars tonight," said Chyna.

"That's right, you said you work what, once a week there?" asked Pharaoh.

"Yeah, don't sound so down, Pharaoh. He'll turn up."

"I know. It's just that everything is ridin' on this."

"I'll call you when I get off work. Maybe you'll let me pay you back by cookin' you a nice dinner."

Pharaoh smiled. "Sounds perfect," he said.

"A'ight. Well, I'll talk to you later."

"Bye." Click.

Pharaoh closed his cell phone and set it on the coffee table. He reached for the remote and turned the TV on. Token walked into the den modeling her new sun dress.

"Where you going all dressed up?" Pharaoh asked examining Token from head to toe.

"Out to celebrate. You and me, come on." Token said, pulling at Pharaoh's arm.

"What are we celebrating?" Pharaoh with the help of Token, rose to his feet.

"I'll tell you over dinner. Change out of the jeans and lets go."

Pharaoh wasn't really in no mood to be celebrating anything, but he didn't want to ruin Token's moment. He took a quick shower, and dug through his suitcase for something to put on.

"Here," said token walking into the den. She handed Pharaoh one of his button up and some slacks.

"I ironed them while you were in the shower."

"You're really excited. What's going on?" Pharaoh asked unfastening his jeans. He tossed them on the sofa and slid into the slacks and crisp button up.

"I'll tell you later."

"A'ight. But I can't eat much, I told my son's mother we'd have dinner tonight." Pharaoh buttoned his last button on his shirt and put a pair of cuff links on to bring out the shirt. Token led the way outside. She bypassed her Explorer and started down the street.

"Where you going?" Pharaoh stopped in front of the truck.

"Just come on," waved Token.

Pharaoh caught up to Token as she crossed the street. "We going to the mall?" asked Pharaoh.

"You don't like surprises, do you?" Token looked at Pharaoh.

"Okay, you got me. I'ma stop with all the questions."

Token cut through Circuit City's parking lot over to Apple Bee's. "Tadaaa! She said, opening her hands wide at the restaurant.

Pharaoh smiled as they walked toward the entrance. He held the door open for Token, as they went in.

"Smoking?" asked the waitress.

"Non," said Token.

"Right this way."

Pharaoh and Token followed the waitress to a small booth for two, she handed them their menus, and said. "I'll be back in a few minutes to take your orders."

"Okay, so it's not much of a surprise. But I thought we'd get out and have a few drinks," said Token.

"Nah, it's cool. I needed to get out and take my mind off the stress. What's this good news of yours?"

"It's really not news. I've just decided to pursue some old goals of mine. You know how sometimes in life we get so caught up living life from day to day, that we lose sight of the things we wanted to do as children."

"I know exactly where you're coming from."

"Yeah, so I'm in a position now to really just focus on me and I'm going to go for it."

"Are you guys ready to order?" the waitress asked, cutting Token short. "Excuse me, darling."

"No, you're okay. Let's see. I'll have the chef salad with grilled chicken slices and extra ranch dressing, with a side of Buffalo wings."

"I'll have the same," ordered Pharaoh. His cell phone lit up and vibrated on his hip. He slid it off the hook of his belt and looked at the screen. "Excuse me, but I have to take this," he told,Token.

"Pharaoh, she's here," said Chyna.

"Who, what are you talkin' 'bout?"

"That girl, Tez's stripper girlfriend. She's here at All Stars…"

Pharaoh sat up. "Is he with her?"

"I don't see him, but he's probably not far behind," Chyna said looking around the club.

"I'm on my way." Click.

Pharaoh looked at Token and said, "I'm sorry, but I have to leave. Something serious just came up."

"It's cool. I'll finish tellin' you later."

"You want me to walk you back home?" Pharaoh slid out the booth.

"I'ma stay and eat, have a few drinks. I'm alright. I'll see you at home later."

"A'ight." Pharaoh turned and rushed out the door and ran back to the house.

Chapter Eleven

Chyna hung up the phone and stepped from behind the bar. She followed Lil' One into the dressing room, she was about ten steps behind her. Lil' One leaned over the steel folding chair digging through her locker. She sat two brochures from Wayne State University on the bench beside her, and pulled out a pair of heels.

Chyna walked over to her own locker, a few lockers down and pretended as if she were freshening up. She sprayed a fine mist of perfume on her right wrist and rubbed her wrists together in a circular motion. She closed the locker, before starting a conversation with Lil' One. "What are you looking to take up?"

Lil' One looked up at Chyna, as if to say you talking to me? "Oh," she said looking down at the brochures. "Business Management!"

"That's good that you're lookin' to do something besides come in here and dance for these niggas every night. My name is Chyna."

Lil' One smiled, then offered her name, "I'm Tameka, but my stage name is Lil' One."

Chyna extended her hand to Lil' One's. Chyna asked at the end of their shake. "So, what are you going into after you finish school?"

"Cosmetology. A friend of mine, we're going to open a shop." Lil' One closed her locker, and then stood up.

Chyna started for the door with Lil' One at her side. "Is that right? You do hair?" asked Chyna.

"Yeah. I've been doing hair since I was maybe sixteen."

"Me too," Chyna said stepping onto the floor of the club.

Maybe you can show me a few of your styles, and we can work on getting' you a chair in the shop." Smiled Lil' One.

"I'd like that. Well, let me get back to work in the meantime. We'll talk more."

"Okay." Lil' One waved her hand at the DJ to crank her anthem, as she slowly climbed the stairs to the stage. Niggas gawked with every step she took. Her ass seemed to vibrate as she reached the top of the stage. "What yo' life like, cause mine's is real." Lil' One swung around the pole then dropped low.

*****

"Hello, Pharaoh?" asked Chyna.

"Did he show up yet?" asked Pharaoh.

"I still don't see him."

"I'm pullin' into the parking lot now. I'ma watch the door, but you call me if he so happens to pop up..."

"Okay. Bye."

Pharaoh bypassed the valet and parked his black 500 SL Benz in the second row. He backed in so that the Benz was facing the front door. Pharaoh cut the car off and looked at the clock on the dash. It was only going on 10 o'clock. 'Plenty of time,' he thought clutching the ass of his .45. He peered through the tinted windshield at the front door. Satisfied that he could see the entire entrance, he leaned his head back against the soft leather headrest, and waited.

It was going on one o'clock, and Pharaoh saw no sign of Tez. His cell vibrated and slid across the dashboard. He caught it before it fell, and flipped it open.

"I don't think he's going to show," said Chyna.

"We still got an hour. What about ole' girl?"

"She just stepped off stage. I believe that was her last set. She's going into the dressing room now. " Chyna watched Lil' One, while twirling the phone cord around her finger.

"This is what I want you to do. Cut into her and tell her that somebody's tryna' hook up with her, but outside the club. I'ma be parked near the entrance, if she goes for it, call me."

"I think that I might be able to swing it." Chyna hung up the phone and walked around the bar. She waited for Lil' One to finish getting dressed. A few moments later, Lil' One came dragging her suitcase on its heels out the dressing room. She waved bye at Chyna and smiled. Chyna stopped pretending she was wiping the counter and approached Lil' One with a smile of her own. "Girl... It seems you have a fan club," said Chyna.

"What you talkin' 'bout?" laughed Lil' One.

"This nigga wants to meet you."

"Who?" Lil' One looked around the club.

"Oh, he's not in here."

"What, he on some stalkin' shit?" Lil' One crunched up her face.

"Nah, it's not like that. I actually know him from a while ago. He used to come to 007. But anyway, he's a good guy. He just doesn't want nobody to be all in his business. He's got cake, girl."

"Where is he?"

"He says that he'll be outside. He's in a black Benz."

"I'ma see what's up with the nigga."

"A'ight, I'll see you later," Chyna said.

Lil' One pulled her case through the packed club and pushed the entrance door open. She stepped out the club and adjusted her eyes to the dim light hanging over the entrance. She peered at the Benz parked sideways directly in front of her.

"She's on her way out," said Chyna.

"A'ight." Pharaoh closed his cell phone and tossed it on the dashboard. He jumped back at the shadow standing at the passenger door. Realizing it must have been Lil' One he popped the locks.

Lil' One opened the door wide and looked in... "Oh, my God! Pharaoh," she said excited as she climbed inside the car and shut the door.

Pharaoh was just as stunned. He swallowed hard and told his self no. 'This can't be the same girl...' he thought.

"What's wrong?" she asked.

"Oh, nothing." Pharaoh tried playing it cool.

"I did not know, Chyna was talkin' about you when she said somebody wanted to meet me. Oh.. I get it. You ain't want Token finding out. You know that girl got a serious thang for you." smiled Lil' One A.K.A. Princess.

Pharaoh played along. "Yeah, I know. But I'm not feelin' her like that. I'm feelin' you."

"You just saying that," gushed Princess.

"I'm serious. I was feelin' you the moment I saw you sittin' on the sofa. Them pretty thighs caught my eye. It took me a while to find you. So, Lil' One that's yo' dance name?"

"Yeah. But you can call me Princess, or Tameka. My real name's Tameka, but everybody calls me Princess."

"What you'd say we go somewhere and kick it?"

Princess looked at her watch it was only 1:20. "Okay, but only for a little while," she said.

"Gotta be home by a certain hour?"

"Something like that. Where we going, so I can follow you?"

"Uh… since you can't stay long, we'll drive over to Rouge Park. How far are you from there? I ain't tryin' have you all out your way…"

"No. That's fine. I'm not too far from Rouge. Just let me put this suitcase in the car." Lil' One reached for the door handle and got out.

Pharaoh watched her through his rear-view mirror. 'Damn,' he thought. He couldn't believe that Princess was Lil' One. The shit blew his mind. 'Tez must ain't tell her about me,' Pharaoh rationalized. 'If I was a rat, I wouldn't want my bitch knowing either.'

Pharaoh saw Lil' One's head lights pop on. He put his car in drive and waited for her to pull behind him. They turned onto 8 Mile and drove three blocks down to Livernois. Pharaoh stayed in his mirrors to make sure Lil' One didn't turn off. He was going to do a U-turn and catch her ass, if she did.

Pharaoh scanned the deserted park as he pulled in. He drove to the farthest corner of the park, then cut his lights off. He parked on the side of the two city dumpsters, and immediately got out. Lil' One cut her engine, then climbed out her Shadow and walked around to the trunk where Pharaoh stood with his hands inside his hoody.

"It's dark out here," said Princess. "We gone get in your car, right?" she asked, assuming Pharaoh wanted to fuck, or at least wanted some head.

He could see the lust in her eyes. "It'll be plenty of time for that later. I just want to kick it and get to know you." Pharaoh raised his arm. "Shall we?" he nodded toward the wood chip trail.

Princess blushed, as she hooked her arm to Pharaoh's. She looked up into his eyes as they started down the trail.

"When I look into your eyes, it's as if I've been knowing you my whole life," said Princess.

"Is that right?" smiled Pharaoh. He was indiscreetly scanning the park for any other pedestrians. There were none.

"Yeah…"

"Maybe you feel that way because I remind you in some way of somebody close to you."

"Let me think… Nah, I can't say that you do."

"What about your boyfriend?"

"Who said I had one?"

Pharaoh, took Princess by the hand and spun her around. Coming to a stop, he said. "You're really expecting me to believe all this is not spoken for?" Pharaoh's eyes rode the curves of Princess calves up to her waist.

"I still don't think you remind me of him in anyway," Princess said, then took a step back into their slow stroll.

"That's because you know nothin' about him. Tez, right?" asked Pharaoh. He stopped to face Princess.

Her face bald up with confusion. "How do you know my boyfriend's name? Pharaoh, what's going on?"

"Tez, never told you about me?" He never told you about his life and why he's hiding?"

"You're scaring me, Pharaoh?"

"Tez, is a snitch. He told on me and my nigga, Ollie, on a conspiracy case. Have you ever met his mom? What about his kids? What's their names, how old are they?"

Princess took a step back, then lashed out because she knew what Pharaoh was saying were true. She didn't know Tez. "You're lying. Tez would never snitch on nobody," she defended.

"No." Pharaoh dug in his pocket and handed Princess the folded picture.

"Where'd you get this?" demanded Princess looking up from the photo of her and her father.

"You know damn well where it came from." Pharaoh pulled his .45 from the slid pocket of his hoody. "I'ma tell you like I told your father, pick up the phone and call Tez." Pharaoh held the gun low pointed for Princess's stomach.

She glared at him. She wondered how long he'd been following her, and if anything he spoke was true. Pharaoh cocked the hammer back and waved the pistol at Princess's purse. Princess gritted her teeth, and then opened her purse wide. She dug deep inside and gripped the handle of her 380. She wrapped her finger around the trigger. "I don't know what you want from me," she said, coming out her purse with her gun. Pharaoh locked eyes on the pistol. Princess got off two quick shots, but missed. Boom!

Boom! She back stepped into the woods, gun still blazing. Boom! Boom!

The last shot grazed Pharaoh's left shoulder as he scrambled for cover behind the park bench. "Fuck!" yelled Pharaoh. 'I can't believe I let this bitch get out on me. I can't let her get away.' thought Pharaoh. He peaked around the bench and into the woods. He could see Princess's red heels trekking in the dark. He stood to his feet and gave chase.

Princess was digging in her purse for her phone. She looked over her shoulder to see Pharaoh at the start of the trail. She scrolled through her call- log down to Tez's name and pushed call. "Come on, answer yo' phone, baby," she said. "Ahii." One of her heels got caught between some twigs and broke off, nearly sending Princess to her face. She stumbled, but kept her stride. "Come on, pick up," she turned around and let off two shots missing Pharaoh by inches. Princess ran deeper into the woods with her cell phone pressed to her ear and her gun in the other hand. She got Tez's voicemail, so she pushed end, then call again. Boom! She let off another round knocking a chunk out of one of the trees.

Pharaoh stopped and took aim with both hands on his pistol. He waited for a perfect shot, and as Princess turned to check the distance between them, Pharaoh squeezed the trigger. Boom! Princess caught the bullet right between her chest. The weeded ground hit her in the face hard as she fell. Her cell phone flew out of her hand, but she still gripped her 380. She struggled to her back as Pharaoh inched forward with his gun on her. Click. Click.

Click. Princess squeezed three empty shots, and then threw her gun out of frustration.

"Bitch, I told your ass," Pharaoh said, as he stood over Princess.

"Fuck you, nigga!"

"That's what yo' daddy said." Boom! Boom! Boom! Pharaoh put three slugs into what was once a flawless face. Princess's brains were scattered over the weeds and rocks.

"Stupid bitch," Pharaoh said looking down at her. He was upset, not that she grazed him, but because now he was back to square one. He reached down and grabbed her purse and dumped it out looking for I.D. He grabbed her license and read its address, which was the same Schaefer address. He tucked it in his pocket, before rummaging through the rest of her belongings for any other forms of identification. He didn't want the police to be able to I.D. her right away. It would buy him some time with Tez.

Pharaoh took one last look at Princess's dead body before leaving. His foot kicked her cell phone in his stride. Pharaoh kneeled down and picked up the phone. It was still ringing.

"Hello, baby," said Tez.

Tez voice sent a chill of hate through Pharaoh's entire body.

"Baby, where you at? Hello?" asked Tez.

Pharaoh pushed the off button, then tucked the phone into his pocket and started back for the trail...

Chapter Twelve

In the short time Ralph had been away in Saginaw, Michigan. He had taken the town over with the weed. He shut down all the local peddlers. Once word hit the streets that Ralph had that 'exclusive', what they called it instead of DRO' – every nigga in Saginaw who smoked weed became loyal customers of Ralph's. He was doing so good with the two weed houses that he refused to sell any other dealers weight. Out of the 250 pounds he took out there, he only had about 100 or so left. Ralph fell in love with the small town and even more so with ole' Maxine. She kept that wet pussy either on Ralph's dick, or in his mouth. That's all he did all day. Sell weed and fuck Maxine. With the seed running low and Detroit lingering in the back of his mind, Ralph knew it wouldn't be long before he had to make a trip back. Today couldn't have been more perfect.

Ralph, with the help of Maxine, bagged up the weed for his two spots. They bagged up enough to satisfy the day's demand. From the living room sofa of Max's two-bedroom apartment, Ralph spoke, "I have to make a run back to Detroit today, baby."

"I wanna come."

"Maybe next time. This is business and I won't be but a couple of days," Ralph said, as he placed one of the complete bags on the small digital scale sitting on the coffee table.

"Bring me something back," said Max, as she did the same, weighing a few of her packaged bags.

"How many we got?" I want to get on the road early." Ralph held a plastic grocery bag open at the edge of the coffee table and scooped the twenty-sack bags into the bag, while mouthing his count.

"This should be enough. If not, I'll bag up some more later," said Max. She scooted across the sofa they shared and climbed on top of Ralph's lap. She wrapped her arms gracefully around his neck then kissed his lips softly. "Hmm…" she moaned, ending the kiss. "You gon' give me some before you hit the road?" she asked pressing her pussy down on Ralph's rising dick.

He was only in his boxers, as she only wore a shot T-shirt and a thong. Ralph palmed both Max's ass cheeks. His fingers sunk deep into the softness of Max's ass. She reached down and pulled him through the hole of his boxers, then slid the front patch of her thong aside and guided Ralph inside her. "Ahh…"

"Shit…" Ralph sighed behind Max. Her glove felt as good as it did the first time they had sex, it was actually getting better with every session.

Max worked Ralph out a nut while sucking on his neck. She could feel him cumming inside her, so she spread her legs farther apart letting Ralph dig deeper.

"Ahh.." he sighed, sliding Max down on his dick one last time before leaning his head back Ralph marinated in the pussy for a few minutes, while Max kissed him over.

"A'ight baby, let me go take a shower so I can get going." Max kissed, Ralph's lips once more, then rose up from his half limp dick. Ralph went to the bathroom to take a five-minute shower. His clothes were spread out across the bed along with a crispy pair of Air Force One's at the foot of the bed. Max was packing some clothes into a suitcase for Ralph as he dressed.

"I'll call you when I hit the city to let you know I made it," Ralph said standing with the front door ajar.

"Be careful, Ralph." Max , rubbed down Ralph's chest and planted a wet two minute kiss on him. She opened her eyes at the end of the kiss and handed Ralph his suitcase.

"In a few…" Ralph smiled, then turned and left. He took the stainless steel staircase down to the parking lot and put the suitcase in the trunk of his Lexus. Ralph hit the horn and waved up at Max who was standing in the window of the apartment. He pulled out the lot and turned on the radio. 94.5 was playing the Oldies but Goodies; The Mighty O'Jays 'For the love of money' was playing. That's exactly how Ralph felt about life. With the exception of Maxine, he had no love for anything else or anyone except money.

Ralph drummed his fingers on the steering wheel as he pulled onto I-94. He got in the fast lane and brought the speed up to 75 mph, then pushed the cruise control button. He leaned his seat back and cracked the sunroof. Ralph couldn't help but think about Pharaoh. He wondered if he found out about Tez's mother being killed. And if he knew who did it. 'P, gotta understand. That bitch-nigga killed Tuff, Robin, Swift and J-Nutty. That was the only family I had.' thought Ralph. He continued in his rationalization while he coasted the highway. He saw the exit sign leading into Detroit. "Fuck it," he said opening his cell phone. He scrolled down to Pharaoh's name and pushed call.

Pharaoh had spent the night at Chyna's apartment. He was too tired to drive home after eating the dinner she had cooked for him, and his thoughts were pre-occupied with killing Tez. Pharaoh's cell phone vibrated against the wooden night stand beside Chyna's bed. It hummed loudly awaking Pharaoh from his light sleep. He reached for the phone and without opening his eyes, he opened its flip and put it to his ear. "Hello," he said dryly.

Ralph hesitated at the sound of Pharaoh's voice.

"Who is this?" Pharaoh asked looking up at the ceiling.

"What up, doe?" Ralph said as if he'd never run off. He waited for a response nervously.

"Ralph?" asked Pharaoh, as he sat up in bed. Knowing that it was him, Pharaoh asked "where you at?"

"On my way to see you," said Ralph. He turned the radio down and listened closely for any hint in Pharaoh's voice that he might be angry. Pharaoh played it cool. "Good. I was worrying that something may have happened to you. I drove pass the house of Rosemary and its all boarded up and shit. I didn't know what happed to ya'll.

"You're not in Canada?"

"Nah, how I'm gon' sit back when ya'll niggas losing the war. I told you you're like my son, family."

Ralph let his guard down. "Where you at my nigga? I'm gon' come holla' at you," said Ralph.. He was turning down Grand River heading east.

Pharaoh looked over at Chyna who was still asleep. He didn't want anybody knowing where his son's mother lived. "Uh, look. Meet me at Eastland Mall in the food-courts in about a half hour," Pharaoh said looking at the alarm clock on the night stand.

"See you in a minute, my nigga." Ralph closed his phone and smiled as he turned the radio back up. His O.G. wasn't mad at him. 'It's all good', so he thought.

Pharaoh sat at the edge of the bed with his back to Chyna. She opened her eyes and said, "You getting' ready to leave?"

"Yeah. Gotta take care of something. But we'll hook up later." Pharaoh stepped into his shoes and fixed the laces. He had slept with his jeans and wife beater on to ensure nothing happened. He hadn't forgotten how soft Chyna was, and he didn't want to find himself lost inside her in the heat of the moment. It would only confuse things right now.

Pharaoh stood, then reached for his white-T and hoody draped over the recliner beside him. He stepped into the bathroom to rinse his mouth with mouthwash and brush his teeth.

"You want me to fix you breakfast before you go?" Chyna propped her head against her hand and watched as Pharaoh tucked his 45 into his pants. "I'm still full from last night, but thank you."

"I'm going to go check on your mom today and see how she's doing. You want me to tell her anything?"

"Just that I love her. And kiss Jr. for me."

"You be safe out there, Pharaoh."

"I'ma call you," said Pharaoh walking out the bedroom. He grabbed the door knob to the front door and snatched it open while he called Maurice.

"Mo, it's me, Pharaoh. I need you to do me a favor and have yo' man run these two numbers and this license plate to see who they came back to."

'Alright. Go ahead," said Mo.

Pharaoh, gave Mo Lil' One's cell and license plate numbers from her car and Tez's number.

"That's it?" asked Mo.

"Yeah. Give me a call when you hear something."

Pharaoh closed his cell and popped the locks as he neared his Benz. He climbed behind the wheel and started the car. Pharaoh plotted on what he was going to do to Ralph for killing Tez's mother. Pharaoh felt like, Tez would have never shot his mom, had Ralph kept it in the street like he told him to. 'Hard headed lil' nigga,' thought Pharaoh as he pushed the 500 SL down the middle lane of 8 Mile. He saw an East Pointe Police car tucked in the median watching for speeders. 'Please don't let this cracker get on me,' he thought looking into his side mirror. Sure enough the cruiser pulled out into traffic and got behind Pharaoh. "Not now. Please not now," said Pharaoh. He checked his speed, and when he looked back up to the mirror the cop was turning off.

Pharaoh let out a deep sigh of relief. He continued on until he reached Kelly Road. He pulled into Eastland Mall's entrance and parked near the Target store in the rear of the mall. He got out and walked through Target into the mall area. Pharaoh had told Ralph to meet him at the mall in order to ease comfort. He could see Ralph sitting at a table in front of the Chinese small section of the food- court.

"You gon' order something, or you gon' just be a mall-rat?" Pharaoh said walking up behind Ralph.

Raph's chair grunted against the tile as he slid back and stood. He smiled while extending his hand. "What up, doe?" he said pulling Pharaoh in for a hug.

They rocked side to side as they continued to embrace.

"Man, I thought that nut got you, too. Step back and let me look at you."

"I'm good," said Ralph.

"Then why you leave?" You ain't tell me shit. You just bounced."

"I had to get away after losing all my niggas. Plus, I felt like I had failed you when you needed me the most."

"Nigga, I can understand that, but no matter what happens we gotta remain one. You feel me?" Pharaoh said, looking Ralph dead in his eyes.

Glad that Pharaoh accepted him back with open arms, Ralph smiled, then said. "I got you my nigga."

Pharaoh wrapped his arm around Ralph's neck and together they walked out of the food-court. "It's us against the world," he said pumping Ralph's head up.

Pharaoh hadn't made any mention about Tez's momma being killed, and Ralph sure in hell wasn't about to bring it up.

"So, what's up, you find the nigga yet?" asked Ralph, as he and Pharaoh walked inside Van Dykes men clothing store.

Pharaoh nodded at the owner and walked to the back and flipped through some racks.

"Not yet but it's definitely in the works." Pharaoh looked up from the racks at Ralph. "I'm going to need your help."

"That's why I'm here."

"A'ight.   What happened with all the DRO' and the money?" Pharaoh changed the subject.

"I have most of the money, but as for the rest of the weed, I don't know. You check the warehouse?"

"Nah. I haven't had time for real. But when this is all over, I know you want to get back in the game."

"No question."

"Let's take care of Tez's rat-ass first, then we'll focus on that. Come on, let's bounce…"

Chapter Thirteen

"You call ya'self runnin' off with some of my money. Well, you betta keep on runnin', bitch. Tez said as if Lil' one was sitting in front of him. He had just finished counting the money he took from Amp for the third time and $72,000 and some change was missing. He figured Lil' One had taken the money and ran off. "Yeah. Run bitch, run… 'cause when I catch you, lights out." Tez stuffed the money back into the garbage bags before reaching for this lighter on the coffee table. He sparked his morning blunt and sat back on the sofa while collecting his thoughts. 'Fuck it. I'ma find me a new bitch and name her, my new bitch,' Tez laughed at the thought. He choked and gagged from the smoke and laughter. "Yeah, that's what I'ma do," he said pushing up from the sofa.

His zebra skin housecoat swished from side to side on his way to the bedroom. He stepped out of his slippers, took off his mink drawers, then tossed the house coat on the bed. Tez went back into killer-mode. He dressed in his usual all black with his signature hoody. The outfit wouldn't be complete without his trusted .40 cal. He reached under his pillow for the gun and tucked it under his hoody. He grabbed about ten pre-rolled blunts and was out the door. He pushed the alarm button to his new 750 BMW. Tez decided to stop through the hood before he went ho' shoppin', as he called it. He wanted to show off his champagne Beemer and show niggas that he wasn't hiding. He pulled into the Sunoco gas station on the corner of 7

Mile and Syracuse after spotting a crap game jumping off near the alley of the station. Heads turned and locked on the 750 as Tez parked at the pump and got out.

"Ah shit…" Floyd said at the sight of Tez.

Niggas started stuffing their pockets out of fear that Tez might hold the game up.

The Arab Baby working inside the station had beat on the window telling Tez to move his car.

"Fuck you!" yelled Tez, giving Baby the finger. "What up, doe?" Tez said reaching the game.

Niggas were on edge. The one hype game where niggas popped slick and bagged it up with big bets, was now a quiet still game.

"Ya'll niggas ain't gotta be scared. I ain't gon' rob ya'll bitch-ass. Not unless I lose," said Tez. He kneeled down and joined the game. "What's the point?" he asked.

"Ten," said Lemon Head. He was on the dice.

"Bet ya' hand you miss it," said Tez.

"You gotta show me some money," said Lemon Head as he shook the dice high above his head. "The last time you came through, you robbed everybody with no gun. Fat Burger's," Lemon Head said shooting at his ten point.

Tez stuck his hand out and caught the dice.

"What you doin'? I'm the fader," John John said leaning down.

"How much is the fade?" asked Tez, still clutching the dice.

"Fifty," said John John.

Tez dug in his pocket and pulled out a large bank roll. He peeled off a fifty and handed it to John John.

"Nah, he was 'bout to go out," said John John.

"Nigga, get yo' bitch-ass outta my fuckin' ear." Tez focused on Lemon Head. "Now bet something," he said.

Lemon Head dropped another fifty to the center and Tez matched him, then tossed him the dice.

Lemon Head picked the dice up. He shook em' high above his head, then short rolled a seven.

"Seven and a loser," teased Tez. He raked the petty change to him. "Come on. Next shotter with a dream," he popped.

"Ole' janky-ass nigga," Lemon Head said under his breath, while wiping the sweat from his forehead with his T-shirt.

"What, ya'll niggas done shootin'?" asked Tez.

Nobody wanted the dice, and nobody would fade Tez's money.

"All ya'll niggas actin' like some faggots," Tez pushed his hand down on the ground to stand himself up. "Mothafucka's lucky. I ain't bring my pistol. I would've robbed all ya'll bitch-ass," Tez said standing to his feet. He took the red dice and launched them over to the top of the gas station. "Buy some more," Tez said as he went to take a step toward his car and Lemon Head stole him from the side.

He caught Tez on the chin, damn near dropping him. Lemon Head kept the punches coming as Tez stumbled backward trying to catch his balance. The first punch still had him dazed.

"Beat his rat-ass!" One of the on-looker's shouted in support of Lemon Head.

Tez shook his head a few times in attempt to shake the daze. His vision was blurred, and then focused in on the fist coming dead at him. He ducked and side stepped. He came out of his waist with ole' trusty and set fire to Lemon Head's chest. Boom!...

He hit Lemon Head five times on his way down and then shot him execution style. Tez spun around and let the last few rounds go at the backs of the rest of the niggas who had been playing dice. They were bolting down the block in every direction. Tez, looked at Lemon Head and said, "What, you think we in the 70's? Niggas don't fight no more."

People were starting to look now that shooting had ceased. Tez tucked his .40 cal. back into his waist, and then casually walked to his car. He backed out the lot and down the wrong way so that no one at the station would get his plate. He swung the car around at the corner of Robinwood and Syracuse and gunned the Beemer down to Ryan Road.

Killing somebody was all in a day's work for Tez. He turned up the radio and leaned his seat back as he brought the speed to a cruise. He sparked an L and nodded to T.I.'s 'King'."

"Sucka's try to play me. I'ma blow em' off the map A.S.A.P," laughed Tez. He came up on 8 Mile and took it down to Hubble. He plucked the short of the blunt out the window as he pulled up in All Stars. He jumped out at the valet booth with the music blasting.

"What up, doe?" said Tez giving the valet a fifty he'd won at the crap game. He hit the door to the club. He stopped under the entrance sign waiting for his intro from the D.J. He looked up at the booth and it was empty, as was the club with the exception of a few dancers and barmaids. The music played low. Tez looked at the clock behind the bar.

It was only going on twelve o'clock. He looked up at Mike's office and the lights were off, which meant he wasn't in yet. Tez flagged two dancers over to his table. Two caramel complexion lil' hot and ready, nothin' special, but decent for the late night. Tez thought to himself as they slid into the booth. 'They ain't all that. But I can work with 'em.'

The girls entered the wrap around booth at opposite ends and scooted close to Tez. He raised his arms above his head and wrapped them around the backs of the girls.

"You don't want us to dance for you?" asked the girl to Tez's right. She gave Tez a sexy under-stare and flashed her small gap as she smiled.

"Nah, I'm good. But I'ma still pay ya'll each song ya'll sit here for," said Tez.

"Shit, that's what I'm talkin' 'bout," the other chick said wiggling closer to Tez.

"Damn, baby girl. Where you from, you sound country as E-mothafucka?" Tez asked tucking his head back at the girl. He noticed one of her eyes was cocked.

"Leave her alone," laughed the other girl. "She's good people," she added.

"I'm sayin' you sound like you from Alabama or somethin.' You're from Alabama, ain't you?" Tez said mocking the girl's accent.

"Forget you," the girl said, rolling her one eye.

"I'm just fuckin' with you. Nah, I called ya'll over here cause I'm doin' interviews."

"For what?" asked the first girl.

"I'ma tell you, but first give me ya'll names, startin' with you," Tez said to cock-eye.

"Lucious."

"What about you?" Tez looked at the other girl.

"Candy. All capitals."

"Both them shits is corny as E-mothafucka. And I'm changing ya'll names."

"You ain't even told us what we gone be doin'," said Candy.

"Listen, let's be real. You hoes ain't makin' no money up in here."

"Who you callin' a hoe?" asked Lucious.

"You know what I mean. Look, I been in here the past two weeks and I ain't seen neither one of ya'll leave outta here with no more than a couple hun'd. And half of that you gotta give to Mike. It's time to get on somethin' new. Startin' with yo' name. That shit is whack and doesn't make me want to spend no money. If you can't make a nigga's dick hard, how you expect to get some money outta him."

"So, what we gon' be doin'?" asked Candy.

"Settin' niggas up. These dope-boys that be in here every night making it rain. We gon' hit their stash. But first, ya'll gotta be able to make em' want you. These nappy-ass weaves," Tez said pulling at the girl's hair. "And these cheap ass outfits. All this shit has gotta go. Niggas gon' spend their money on something only if it makes him feel like money. So, ya'll gotta look like money. I know you hoes is scratching and surviving, so I'ma do something I usually don't do. I'ma pay to get ya'll hair and nails done.

Then I'ma give you hoes a Jenny Jones make-over with a new wardrobe, dust you bitches off."

"Shit. I'm with that," said Candy.

Tez looked at Lucious. "What about you, you in?" he asked.

"Yeah," said Lucious.

"A'ight. Ya'll hoes go and get dressed, so we can get going. I'ma sit out here and try and think of ya'll new names. Rich now, ya'll just my New Bitches…" laughed Tez.

"What about, Mike? We can't just leave," said Lucious.

"I got Mike. Just go and get ready."

Candy and Lucious scooted out the booth and raced into the dressing room excited. Tez sparked a blunt and plotted on how he'd have the two setting niggas up in no time. Lil' One hadn't crossed his mind.

Chapter Fourteen

Stacy had been blowing Pharaoh's cell up all day, every day. He hadn't returned any of her calls because he wasn't ready to deal with all her questions; when can I see you? Why are you doing me like this? etc... Pharaoh really felt like Stacy was only blowing him up because he was still on the loose. Had he gone to jail for life, all that sweating would cease.

Pharaoh needed to get word to Ollie, though, and let him know he hadn't forgotten about him. Pharaoh dictated a letter to Ralph who sat at the kitchen table of his apartment, while Pharaoh paced the floor and talked with his hands. "Write this," he said.

Dear Ollie:

My dude, I know you're thinking that I done forgot about you and I could see why. But know that what we discussed is on the grill and is almost done. As far as ole' girl, shit ain't what it used to be. Basically, the lick is burnt out. But I dropped your O.G. off some dust to put on your books.

I'm just hollerin' at you. You'll be on the bricks in no time. So don't ever believe you're in the land of the forgotten, cause I'm out here pushing to bring you home. Until then, my nigga. Stay up!
One Love.

"You want me to put a name at the bottom?" asked Ralph.

"Nah, just in case they got him on mail monitoring. They can't say who the letter came from. Seal that boy up and put a stamp on the envelope," directed Pharaoh.

While he was dictating the letter to Ralph, he missed a call, a call that he'd been waiting on for two days. Pharaoh pushed the call button on Mo's name and waited as the phone rang.

"Yeah," answered Maurice."

"Give me some news I can use," said Pharaoh.

"Well, I don't know if you'll be able to use it. Both numbers are to cell phones. And the billing address was at some phone shops. As for the plate, the plate came back to Tameka Hanson, on 2300…"

"Schaefer…" Pharaoh finished Mo's sentence. His voice spelled disappointment. "I was afraid that was the address," he said.

"Well, if you get anything else, give me a holla. I'll be at the shop."

"A'ight," said Pharaoh. He looked down at the floor in a daze, as he closed his cell shut.

"What's up, P? Everything good?" asked Ralph. He was folding Ollie's letter and had noticed the look of dismay on Pharaoh's face. Pharaoh just shook his head. He waited two days for that worthless information. Pharaoh wiped his face but the sudden stress remained in place.

"Who was that?" asked Ralph.

"Mo." All this time we been sittin' here waitin' on this nigga to call, and he got the same info we got."

"So, back to the drawing board."

Pharaoh looked at Ollie's letter on the table. He knew what had to be done. "Nah… It's all or nothin'," he said, grabbing his car keys and Ollie's letter off the table. "Come on, we out," said Pharaoh.

Pharaoh went into another one of his zones. He knew one way for certain to find Tez, but it was complicated. 'Everything rides on this. It's Ollie or her. Fuck that. It's me or her.' Pharaoh told himself. No further deliberation was needed. Pharaoh stretched out and gripped the wheel with one hand. He pushed the Benz down 7 Mile making a quick stop at the post office on Caldwell. He handed Ralph the letter and watched as he slid the letter inside the mailbox.

Ralph climbed back in the car and closed the door. "Where we going, my nigga?" he asked.

"Holla at this chick. When we get there, I don't want you saying nothin' besides hello."

"Why, what's up?"

"Just follow my lead…"

Pharaoh took 7 Mile to Kelly Road and made the turn around through one of the medians. He drove two blocks down then pulled in the driveway behind Token's Explorer. He saw the curtain to the house brush back. 'Damn,' he thought. He hadn't finished gathering his thoughts. Token swung the door open and was standing on the small landing of the porch.

"Come on," said Pharaoh pulling his door handle.

Token didn't look her normal perky self. She stood with her arms folded, and she was still in her night clothes.

"Token. This is my boy Calvin," Pharaoh said introducing Ralph.

Token nodded at Ralph, then focused on Pharaoh. "I've been callin' you for the past two days. Why you ain't pick up yo' phone? You had me thinking that something happened," said Token.

"That's my bad. I was dealing with something."

Token turned around and led them into the house. Ralph playfully tapped Pharaoh at the sight of Token's ass scrambling inside her silk pajama pants. It was obvious she wasn't wearing any panties. Pharaoh gritted his teeth and mouthed the word 'stop.'

Token stopped at the sofa and flopped down with her arms still folded.

"You missed me that much, or is something else bothering you?" Pharaoh asked taking a seat close to Token.

"It's Princess. I haven't heard from her in a few days," said Token.

Pharaoh's stomach did a flip. His right brow rose with eagerness.

"It's not like her to go days without calling me. I can't get her on her cell or at the apartment."

'Apartment?' thought Pharaoh. 'Keep talkin,' he thought.

Token unfolded her arms and turned to face Pharaoh. She put her hands on his lap, then spoke. "I think something is wrong, Pharaoh."

"Maybe she's outta town," suggested Pharaoh.

"She would've told me. I know what it is. It's her crazy-ass boyfriend."

"What, you think he did something to her?"

"I hope not. Can you please take me to check on her in case his crazy-ass is there?"

"I'll do that. But who is this dude, what's his name?" Pharaoh watched Token lips in slow motion. He damn near bust a nut as she said the million dollar name.

"Tez…"

"Yeah, we'll take you," said Pharaoh.

Token hugged his neck, and then kissed the side of his face. She jumped from the sofa and cut the corner toward the staircase. "Le t me get dressed!" she yelled on her way up.

Pharaoh wasted not a second. He bolted for the den. He snatched at the closet's door handle and grabbed his two Louis Vutton luggage and Stacy Adams bag. He raced them out to Ralph and gave him the keys to the Benz. "Put these in the trunk. Hurry up," he said closing the door behind Ralph.

Things were going to be a lot easier than Pharaoh expected. He wasn't going to have to threaten Token for Princess's address, she was about to willingly take him there.

"I'm ready," said Token after reaching the bottom step into the hallway. She met Pharaoh at the front door. "We taking my truck or your car?" she asked.

"I'll drive," Pharaoh needed the comfort of the tinted windows.

Pharaoh made Ralph sit in the backseat behind Token, while she gave him the directions.

"What you know about this nigga, Tez?" asked Pharaoh, looking over at Token. She was trying to call Princess…

"Nothin', except that he's crazy," she said closing her phone.

"Crazy, how?"

"I can look in a person's eyes and can tell if they got em' all. That nigga ain't all the way there. His eyes are blank."

Pharaoh met eyes with Ralph through the rear-view and nodded. 'That's Tez,' he thought.

"Nah, I was just asking cause I wanted to know if me and my nigga needed to bring our guns."

"Hell, yeah… That's why I asked you to come."

Pharaoh used the rest of the drive to get his plan together. He cranked up the radio. Ole' James Brown was in mid-play "You sold me out… gotta get ready for the big payback."

Pharaoh clutched his iron as James said. He was gettin' ready for the big payback.

"It's on your left coming up," Token pointed to the entrance of the apartment complex. It was hidden behind an array of bushes.

Pharaoh hit his blinker, then slowed the Benz and made a left into the complex.

Token kept her finger pointed. "Pull around here. I don't see her car."

Pharaoh parked in the empty space and surveyed the buildings. "Where's the apartment?" he asked Token.

"In that building right there." Token said with her head down. She was digging in her purse. "Come on, I have a key," she said opening her door and getting out.

Pharaoh cut the car off, and then looked in the backseat at Ralph. "You know the business."

Ralph nodded before pulling the door handle. Pharaoh and Ralph both put their hoodies on their heads and tailed Token up the two flights of steps. They stood back while she opened the entrance door. She pulled the door handle and held it open for Pharaoh and Ralph.

"It's just around the corner. Right here," Token said about to stick her key in the lock.

"Hold on," said Pharaoh pulling out his .45, as did Ralph. He brandished his 357 magnum. Pharaoh nodded toward the door and Token quietly unlocked the two locks then gently twisted the knob. Pharaoh brushed past Token with Ralph on his heels. They stepped in the apartment guns raised high, waving them side to side. Pharaoh started down the hall and nodded at Ralph for him to check the first door on the left. He kept down the hall and slowed as he approached the half opened door on his right. He cocked the hammer back then leaned his shoulder into the door pushing it open wide.

Pharaoh pointed his gun at the bed, and slowly lowered it to his side. The room was empty. Ralph joined him in the bedroom, where Pharaoh probed through the dresser drawers.

"It's empty. The front room, too," informed Ralph.

"What are you doing? Put those back," Token said taking the papers from Pharaoh and placing them back inside the dresser drawer.

Ralph raised his eyebrows at Pharaoh, like what's up? Pharaoh shook his head no. 'Not yet, anyway,' he thought.

"I was just tryin' to see if I knew this nigga, Tez you talkin' about," said Pharaoh, as to explain why he had been probing.

"I guess you were right. Maybe they did go out of town, and she just didn't tell me. I mean, everything looks normal," said Token.

"Yeah," Pharaoh accented, still probing with his eyes. The ashtray on the night stand was filled with roaches. That verified it for Pharaoh that Tez was living there. That and the fifth of Remy Martin V.S.O.P. tucked on the side of the bed. That was Tez's stee-low, Remy and blunts...

Come on, let's go back out front. I'ma write Princess a quick note, then we can go," said Token, leading the way out of the room.

Pharaoh snooped around the living room while Token was at the kitchen counter penning Princess a note.

"Okay, I'm ready," said Token. She took a magnet off the fridge and posted her note.

Pharaoh reluctantly followed Token out the apartment. The only good thing about it was that he wouldn't have to kill her now. Pharaoh had it already mapped out. After he killed Tez, he was gonna stank Token. He wasn't taking any chances on leaving no witnesses.

Chapter Fifteen

Tez was parked outside Impressions Hair Salon on 8 Mile and Ryan. He was smoking a blunt, while he waited on Lucious and Candy. They had already done their shopping, and were getting the finishing touches to their Jenny Jones makeover.

Tez sat up and popped the locks when he saw Lucious and Candy stepping through the adjacent glass corridor. They smiled from ear to ear as they approached the car. Candy was pulling at the passenger door handle.

"Open the door," she said.

"Get in the back," Tez waved her around to the back of the car.

"You trippin' why we gotta sit in the back?" Lucious asked from the back seat.

"See, that's what's wrong with you hos now, a nigga give you an inch and you want a mile. Baby steps," Tez said turning around in his seat to face the girls. "Okay, now ya'll lookin' like a lil' money. Just let me fix this... yeah, keep that over that eye. You don't' want to scare a nigga off," Tez pushed the side of Lucious hair over her cock eye.

"Where we going now?" asked Candy.

"We gonna kick it at my spot. Just chill for the night, cause tomorrow it goes down. We gonna go over some things, then we gonna do some thangs," said Tez flicking his tongue at Candy and Lucious through the rear-view mirror.

"You so nasty," laughed Candy.

"Nah, I'ma take it easy on ya'll. I ain't tryna sweat ya' perms out."

Tez, took Lucious and Candy out to the apartment. He had absolutely no regard whether or not Lil' One had decided to come home. It hadn't crossed his mind.

"You hos take ya'll shoes off," said Tez opening the door and stepping inside the apartment. "Make ya'll self's comfortable. I'ma step in the bedroom for a minute."

"Girl, this nigga got us up in some bitch apartment," said Candy.

"I was thinking the same thing. Look at the way it's decorated. Nigga's ain't shit. I tell you," Lucious said taking a seat on the crème leather sofa.

"Look at these," Candy picked up a photo album from the top of the entertainment system. She flipped through the flicks as she took a seat next to Lucious.

"Hold on, go back," Lucious flipped the plastic covered picture back one. She looked at the photo close to her good eye. "That's ole' girl from All Stars…. what's her name, Lil' One."

"Sho' is," Candy agreed.

Tez dug in the fridge for a fifth of ice cold Remy Martin V.S.O.P. He already had his evening blunt sparked and about a quarter smoked. He walked through the small entrance way leading into the living room.

"Ya'll ain't naked yet?" he asked stopping on the side of the sofa. He took a swig from his Remy, and then hit the L.

Lucious and Candy were in tears from laughing so hard.

"Fuck wrong with you silly bitches? Oh, ya'll laughing at my housecoat?" Tez looked down at his get-up.

"What is that you got on?" Candy cracked up.

"Girl, he got on some gorilla drawers," laughed Lucious. She was laughing so hard her legs were raised off the floor, knees in her stomach.

"I ain't stuntin' ya'll," said Tez. He flopped down between them. He sat his fifth on the table and took one last pull, then put the roach in the ash tray.

Candy untied the purple scarf from around Tez's head and wrapped it around her neck. She pulled on its ends, making it stretch side to side.

"Take these off," ordered Lucious, pulling at Tez's mink drawers.

He lifted up a little and allowed Lucious to pull the drawers down around his ankles. She wrapped her hair around her ear, while she jacked Tez's long limp dick. It swelled up from the sensual attention Lucious was giving it. She licked around the head, exciting it more. She could see the veins protruding through the thickness of Tez's dick, and knew that he was geeked up. Lucious sucked down on the head of Tez's dick and tightened her lips, so that they fit like a pussy. With that same tightness, she began skulling Tez.

He leaned back and closed his eyes. Candy stripped down ass naked, before climbing on top of Tez's face. She grabbed the back of his black bald head with one hand and rubbed the small rolls with her fresh French manicured nails, helping guide Tez to her satisfaction. Tez's eyes remained closed while he glazed Candy's clit with his long tongue. He licked up and around her in a firm circular motion.

"Hmm," moaned Candy. It was getting good to her. Tez reached up and palmed her ass cheeks. He used his grip to help press his tongue more firmly against her clit. Candy's knees were starting to buckle, and Tez was determined to take her where she needed to go. He started dipping his head with every circle to ensure he kept his rhythm. Both of Candy's legs shook as she closed her eyes and tilted her head back to the ceiling. Her mouth opened to a silent scream, as her lips swelled.

"Ahh! Ahh…" she hit a high note, as she reached the point of no return.

Tez held her up from falling while she came – came- and kept cumin…

Candy pulled away from Tez's tongue, she was on the brink of pulling her hair out because the multiple orgasms wouldn't stop. She dropped beside Tez on the sofa, legs still trembling and cum running down her thighs.

Tez pulled Lucious up from his dick, and gave her the same spine tingling head game. He wanted them nice and wet before he finally stuck his dick in them.

Chapter Sixteen

It was killing Pharaoh that he hadn't killed Tez yet. He was itching to get back to the apartment, so he could get it over and done with. 'Kill the nigga and move on with my life. This shit has gone on too long as it is', thought Pharaoh. He couldn't even enjoy the peppered steak and shrimp fried rice he was chewing.

Pharaoh had treated Token to some Chinese take-out. He told her it was the least he could do after skipping out on their last dinner. Pharaoh's real reason was because he was stalking Token's house keys. Her key ring had Tez's apartment key on it and he needed it.

"Are you in for the night?" Pharaoh asked, Token as he stood from the dining room table and walked into the kitchen.

"Yeah," said Token closing the fridge. "Why, what's up?" she asked setting the fresh pitcher of kiwi-strawberry Kool-Aid on the table.

"Let me help you with that," Pharaoh unscrewed the lid and poured Token some Kool-Aid into her glass.

"Nah, I wanted to use your truck. I gotta move some thangs in the morning," Pharaoh said pouring himself a glass.

"I ain't got nowhere to be. Not until the late afternoon. You can get it."

"I'ma leave you my car just in case."

"Okay. I'm full. Thank you, that was right on point," said Token.

"Yeah. I'm full, too. I'ma put the rest of this in the fridge and fuck with it tomorrow." Pharaoh pushed his chair back and stood up.

"You done, my man?"

Ralph nodded with a mouth full of Egg Fu Yung.

"You don't talk much, do you?" Token smiled at Ralph.

"Nah, he's like a monk. Just watches and observes," Pharaoh said from the kitchen. He stuck the Styrofoam trays and white boxes of rice onto the shelves and closed the door of the fridge.

"Come on. We out," he told Ralph pushing his chair in. Pharaoh picked Token's key ring up and put it in this pocket, then set his down on the table,

"You getting ready to leave me? I'ma be bored," said Token.

"Yeah. But we'll do something tomorrow when you get done handling yo' business."

"Okay. Give me a hug," said Token.

Pharaoh leaned down and wrapped Token's small frame into his chest. He kissed the top of her head, like a little sister.

"A'ight, I'm out. Call me if you need something."

Token got up to let Pharaoh and Ralph out. "Tomorrow," she said before closing the door.

Pharaoh dug in his pocket for Token's array of keys. He hit the lock button on the key chain as he and Ralph cut across the grass. They climbed in the truck and Pharaoh cranked the engine. He pulled out onto Kelly Road. The tires screeched a little as he made a right on State fair. Pharaoh was trying to get as far away from Token's crib and fast as he could before she realized she hadn't taken her house keys off.

"You ready, lil' nigga?" Pharaoh looked over at Ralph.

Ralph pulled his chrome trey-pound-seven from his waist and held it up. Its chrome gleamed as the street light on the corner of 7 Mile and Hayes shone in the truck. "Am I ready... huh?" chuckled Ralph.

"We gonna get this nigga done and get the fuck up outta there," Pharaoh said leaning his seat back and adjusting his mirrors.

"What if he still not there?"

"We gon' lay."

"This for Tuff, Robin, J-Nutty and Swift," said Ralph as he tucked his 357 back in his waist.

"That nigga shoulda' been dead long time ago, but we gon' put an end to his run tonight." Pharaoh crossed 8 Mile heading into the suburbs.

"Put yo' belt on," he told Ralph as he cruised down Groesbeck.

Pharaoh killed his lights as he pulled the truck up to the entrance of the complex's parking lot. He scanned the dark lot for a space. He parked next to a champagne colored BMW. Ralph went to get out the truck but Pharaoh grabbed his arm.

"Hold up. Let me take the plate off in case we got some nose mothafucka lookin." Pharaoh reached across Ralph's lap and pulled the latch to the glove box. He shuffled around for something he could use to take the plate off. His hand stopped after touching the cool steel of a letter opener. Pharaoh grabbed the small stainless steel letter opener, and then climbed out the truck. He walked around the back and squatted at the center of the hatch. He used the nose of the opener to unscrew the four flat-head screws.

"Come on," he said opening the driver's side door. He tucked the plate under the seat, and snatched the keys from the ignition.

"Don't slam the door," whispered Pharaoh.

Ralph held the handle while he slowly closed the door shut, enough so that the dome light went off. Ralph fell in step with Pharaoh, both pulling their hoodies over their heads. Pharaoh looked up at the buildings. There were a lot of lights still on, which meant people were still awake. Pharaoh's palms became sweaty and his heart raced faster with every step he climbed up the two flights of steps. The anticipation of killing Tez was building. Pharaoh's entire body started sweating. He fumbled with the array of keys at the entrance door trying them all. Just his luck, it was the last key on the ring to open the door.

Ralph pushed off the wall where he stood with a watchful-eye. He stepped inside the building behind Pharaoh and together they inched down to the end of the hall. Pharaoh peaked around the corner down t the apartment. He looked back at Ralph. "Look, this what we gon' do…"

*****

Tez had moved the party to the bedroom. He was back there trying out all Lil' One's toys on Lucious and Candy.

"That looks like it hurts," Candy said of the foot-long of beads. They started out small and got bigger each bead.

"Where that go?" asked Lucious.

Tez was rubbing KY-jelly over the pink beaded cord. "Roll over and I'ma show you," he said helping Lucious onto her stomach. Tez arched her back so that her pussy poked out. He gave it a kiss, then took the start of the beads and penetrated Lucious's tight brown ass hole. Tez watched her nails dig down into the sheets. She moaned as Tez used his free hand to spread her ass cheeks and push the second bead deeper inside. Candy licked around the cord as it crept inside Lucious's ass. Tez was getting off on just the pain alone. Seeing Lucious squirm and her eyes roll to the back of her head made Tez's dick leak. He pulled the beads out and replaced them with the head of his dick.

"Shit…" sighed Tez as he began slow stroking Lucious.

Candy, was spreading Lucious's ass cheeks for Tez, while she licked around the asshole.

*****

Pharaoh turned the knob on the door slowly, then inched the door open. He let Ralph inside the apartment first, as he quietly shut the door. They both held their guns at shoulder level. Ralph looked at the clothes on the sofa and the shoes sitting by the front door. They weren't there when he and Pharaoh had left earlier, he thought.

"Ahh… Fuck me!"

Pharaoh nodded toward the back of the apartment. He cocked the hammer back on his .45 and started down the hall with Ralph hugging the opposite wall.

"Ahh… Oh. Oh." The moans got louder as Pharaoh got closer to the bedroom.

The door was ajar and Pharaoh could see the shadow of a man against the wall. He was pumping a woman from the back. Pharaoh met eyes with Ralph, and dipped his shoulder into the door pushing it wide open. The slam of the door caused Candy, Lucious and Tez to all jump. Tez's eyes locked on the barrel of the .45, and then traveled up the sleeve of the blue hoody.

"What ya'll call ya' self robbin' me?" asked Tez. He automatically thought that Candy and Lucious set him up. "You funky ass bitches. Ya'll set me up," he said sliding out of Lucious.

Pharaoh pulled his hood off his head and watched as Tez's eyes bucked. That was exactly what Pharaoh needed to see, fear!

"Come on, P. We family. Fuck that shit with the feds. I only did that so they'd let me go. I wasn't going to testify on ya'll," said Tez.

"And I'm 'pose to believe that?" asked Pharaoh. He wanted to so bad, but he couldn't let emotion keep him from regaining what he'd been chasing for so long, his life.

"I swear. That's why I went on the run," Tez said inching toward the top of the bed. "Come on, my nigga. You know I'm not a rat. I thought you had set me up by sending me to pick up the work in the first place. Outta all the times you copped, you ain't never took me with you. Then the one time you sent me to pick up the work, the feds jump out on me. I was the one puttin' all the work in, moving niggas out the way."

"Yeah, but you violated in a major way. We can never be dawgz again. It's over." Pharaoh had the trigger about half way pulled back, when Tez made his move. He kicked Lucious in her ass, sending her crashing off the bed into the first bullet from Pharaoh's gun. Her head blew back and her body slumped to the floor.

Tez gripped the ass of his .40 cal. underneath the pillow. He tried to pull the gun from under the pillow, but Ralph put two slugs in his chest. Boom! Boom!

Tez lay flat on his back with his arm stretched under the pillow. He was moving his head slow from side to side. Pharaoh stepped around the side of the bed and pressed the barrel of his gun to Tez's temple.

"Kill me bitch!" yelled Tez.

Those were his last words. Pharaoh yanked the trigger back three times. Boom! Boom! Boom! Three blistering gashes covered the left side of Tez's face. His brains were splattered all over the bed and Pharaoh's hoody. Boom! Ralph gave Candy a single dome shot as she laid on the bed with her eyes closed, hoping that they'd forget to kill her.

It was finally over. Ralph walked around the side of the bed and put his arm around Pharaoh's neck. "Come on, my nigga. It's over," he said pulling Pharaoh with him.

Pharaoh couldn't help but shed a tattoo tear on his way out the apartment. Killing Tez was like killing his blood brother. It was the worst feeling in the world. Even after all the pain and heartache Tez had caused Pharaoh, he still had love for the nigga. Revenge wasn't Pharaoh's reasons for killing Tez, it came down to his life for his. 'Going All Out,' Pharaoh told himself from the passenger seat. He was too distraught to drive, so he had Ralph drive them back to his apartment.

Ralph parked the truck on the street across from his apartment. "Come on, my nigga. We here," said Ralph getting out.

Pharaoh pulled the door handle and met Ralph in the middle of the street. He looked up at Ralph's building. Most of the lights to the apartment were off. 'Good,' he thought Pharaoh stopped once they reached the sidewalk in front of Ralph's building. He grabbed Ralph's arm spinning him around.

"What up?" asked Ralph, looking down the block as if someone were coming.

Pharaoh took a step back and raised his .45 to Ralph's face.

"P. Fuck is you doin'? You know I ain't gon' say nothin' 'bout you killin Tez," said Ralph. His voice cracked with fear.

"This ain't got nothing to do with that. What you didn't think I was going to find out you killed Tez's momma?"

"P, that nigga killed all my niggas."

"Yeah, but I told you not to bring his moms into it. Don't you know my mom is laid up in the hospital with one lung cause Tez tried to kill her. That would've never happened had you not killed his ole' bird."

"My bad, Pharaoh, man. I swear it won't happen again," Ralph said crying.

"I know it won't."

"Come on, P. Look at my stomach." Ralph slowly raised his shirt. "Nigga, I got shot while I was in Wisconsin tryna' push yo' weed. I damn near died. But I kept it from you cause I didn't want to let you down. I done lost all my niggas fighting yo' war. And you gon' kill me? Come on, P. This ain't for us," pleaded Ralph.

"Yeah, but you don't listen. And I can't have no nigga around me who doesn't listen." Pharaoh closed his eyes as he squeezed the trigger. Boom!

Pharaoh, heard Ralph's body hit the ground… He opened his eyes and looked down at the blood seeping from Ralph's forehead onto the sidewalk. Pharaoh did the sign of the cross and asked God to forgive him. He prayed that would be the last time he had to kill someone. He crossed back over to the truck and climbed behind the wheel. He drove down to the end of the block with his lights out and made a left turn.

Chapter Seventeen

Chyna rolled over in bed and felt around for the snooze button on the sounding alarm clock. She found it and then rolled onto her back. Still fighting the call of sleep, Chyna told herself 'get up.' Reluctantly, she pulled the sheets off her body and sat up in bed. She swung her legs around the side of the bed and placed her feet into her slippers.

Chyna used the bathroom, and then walked towards the living room to go check the mailbox. She saw Pharaoh lying on the long sofa with his shoes and clothes on. He had his hoody pulled low over his eyes. "Good morning," he said, as he pulled his hoody back.

"When did you get here?" asked Chyna.

"Late last night."

"You could've come and got in the bed."

"I got him…"

"What?"

"I got him. It's over," Pharaoh said, then stood up. He walked over to Chyna and gave her a hug.

"Are you okay?" asked Chyna, knowing how hard Pharaoh must have been taking it.

"Yeah… I'm alright," said Pharaoh, looking Chyna in the eyes. "Now I can get back to living my life and stop running."

"What are you about to do, turn yourself in?"

"Not yet. I still got a few things that I need to square away before I do that, but I'm in the clear." Pharaoh let out a deep sigh of relief.

Chyna folded her arms and analyzed Pharaoh's face. She knew what he meant when he said he had to square some things away.

"What's wrong?" asked Pharaoh.

"You're going to see her, aren't you?"

Pharaoh stared blankly at Chyna. He dropped his stare to the floor, then said, "It's something I've gotta do in order to move on. It's been on my mind heavy." Pharaoh looked back up at Chyna.

"When are you leaving?"

"Today, but I wanted to see you before I left to let you know that it's over. When I get back, we're going to work on that salon I promised you. So, get all your decorations together." Pharaoh cracked a smile. However, Chyna wasn't as enthusiastic.

"Be safe," she said walking Pharaoh to the front door.

Pharaoh kissed Chyna's forehead, then wiped the side of her face with the back of this hand. "I will," he said. "Kiss Jr. for me."

"Okay," Chyna said dryly. She was a little hurt because she was beginning to think that there might have been a chance for her and Pharaoh, but it was clear that's not what he wanted. Chyna couldn't even look at him, as she stood with the door ajar.

Pharaoh caught the vibe. He didn't say anything; he just turned and walked away. The sound of Chyna closing the door was like a chapter of Pharaoh's life closing. The resentment he once harbored toward Chyna for having Jr. without his permission was no more. He took a deep breath and kept his stride down the hall. He stepped out of the building into the warm morning sun and exhaled. 'Life,' he thought. Pharaoh climbed behind the wheel of Token's Explorer and cranked the engine. He cracked the windows and then backed out.

He cut the radio on to 98.7 and Pac's 'That's just the way it is' was in mid-play. He stretched out with one hand gripping the wheel and the other arm propped against the center console. Pharaoh leaned to the side as he cruised the truck down 7 Mile Road. He was collecting his thoughts when a Detroit police car pulled alongside of him. The light on the corner of Hoover caught them, and Pharaoh casually looked down at the young white officer staring up at him from the passenger seat of the cruiser. Pharaoh smiled at the officer, and then focused back on the road. He had not a worry in his body. They could've pulled him over and took him to jail right then, and it wouldn't have made one bit of a difference. He watched the black and gold squad car make a left on Barlow.

Pharaoh took 7 Mile to Kelly Road., and drove down two blocks to Token's house. He pulled into the driveway and honked the horn. He cut the truck off then climbed out. Token was standing in the door as Pharaoh cut across the lawn. "Good morning," he said with a smile, while climbing the three steps up to the landing.
"It must be a beautiful morning," Token said smiling back at Pharaoh. "I have never seen you smile before. What's

going on?" Token asked opening the screen and holding it open for Pharaoh.

"I just woke up on the right side of the bed this morning, I guess." Pharaoh stopped in the center of the living room.

"Let me fix you some breakfast then." Token started for the kitchen.

"Nah, I can't stay. I just came to drop your truck off and to thank you."

"You're welcome. You can use that old thang anytime you want."

"Nah. I mean thank you for opening your door and arms to a nigga when I really needed it. I appreciate it," said Pharaoh.

"You talkin' like this will be the last time I'll see you."

"I wouldn't say that, but it will be for a minute. I'm getting ready to deal with my past and stop runnin'."

"You 'bout to turn yourself in?" Token asked moving closer to Pharaoh.

"In a week or so. I've gotta handle a few more things before I do. I just wanted to let you know that you'll always be my people."

"I hate to see you go," Token softly said.

"Come here," Pharaoh said opening his arms. He hugged Token tightly.

She reached her hands up to the side of Pharaoh's face, and pulled him into her lips. She allowed just her lips to touch, but after Pharaoh didn't refuse her, token kissed around his mouth gently. She eased her tongue into his mouth and enjoyed a minute long kiss.

"I had to get that off before you left. I've been holding that in since the first time we met," said Token.

Pharaoh didn't say anything. He just flashed his cool smile. Had it not been for Mo, he would have fucked Token a while back.

Token walked Pharaoh to the front door and gave him his keys. "You take care and don't be no stranger. If you have to do some time, you already know I'll come to see you."

"I'd like that. Well, let me get going." Pharaoh kissed the side of Token's face, then walked down the three steps. He hit the alarm button to his 500 SL parked at the curb. He opened the door and climbed behind the wheel. He hit the horn and Token waved him off from the porch. Pharaoh sighed as he drove down Kelly Road. 'Another chapter closed,' he thought. He stopped by Al's Barber shop to holla at Mo. He was greeted by all the playas and hustlas alike as he stepped through the door. They respected the fact he hadn't sold his soul in the face of adversity. There was nothing but respect being shown to Pharaoh. He thanked all them, then excused himself and Mo to the back room.

"Can't get right," Mo said closing the door behind him.

"Well, I guess you finally got right. Boy, I remember when you was just a kid runnin' errands and soaking up game."

Pharaoh and Mo took a seat on two bar stools around the crap table.

"Yeah. I remember," Pharaoh said smiling. He could still see himself cleaning up the shop and playing close attention to all the hustlas.

"So, you got his ass, huh?" asked Mo.

"You don't miss nothin'."

"It's the barber shop. What do you expect? Plus they showed it on the News."

"Yeah, it's over. But I'ma need your help with one more thing."

"Anything," said Mo.

Chapter Eighteen

Pharaoh had been standing in line for nearly twenty minutes. He checked his watch, and then let out a sigh of frustration. His flight was scheduled to leave in less than ten minutes, and the old white couple in front of him was arguing with the red head working behind the counter. The old man wanted a refund because his flight had run out of peanuts.

Pharaoh wanted to kick the old bastard square in his ass. Out of the twenty minutes he'd been waiting, the couple spent eighteen of them arguing about nothing. 'I hope, I'm not like that when I get old,' Pharaoh thought as the couple finally moved on. Pharaoh stepped to the counter of the Metro Airport and gave the woman the alias Maurice head set everything up in. The clerk typed the name into her computer, and then smiled up at Pharaoh. She waited as the automated machine to her right spit Pharaoh's first-class ticket out, before handing it to him.

"Have a nice flight," she told him.

Pharaoh nodded and returned the gesture with a closed smile. He reached down for his carry-on luggage and walked over to the waiting area for his departure. The terminal's intercom system crackled and Pharaoh's flight number was announced. 'That be me,' he said to himself awaiting the opening of the door leading to the ramp.

A woman appeared at the wood-framed podium and began checking ticket stubs. She waved Pharaoh on board with a closed smile. He was ushered to first-class by a petite yellow-bone flight attendant, where he slid into a window seat.

"Can I get you anything?" asked the attendant.

"Maybe later," Pharaoh said smiling. He leaned his seat back and folded his arms. Pharaoh watched the seats fill with passengers; each face had a story to tell. Pharaoh's included.

Pharaoh closed his eyes and smiled, as he went back down memory lane. He remembered sitting in the crack house with Tez and Ollie grindin', while watching 'New Jack City': Those were hard times, but they were also the simple times. Pharaoh thought back on the bank robbery, then getting into a shoot-out with the police, and going to Arizona for the first time. That was his first time ever leaving the city of Detroit, on the run.

Pharaoh opened his eyes at the sound of the plane's engine roaring. He watched as the plane raced down the run-way and pull up into the sky.

*****

Pharaoh's plane landed at the Freeport Air terminal in Phoenix, Arizona. It was only 1:00 in the afternoon, and the weather was already in the low 100's. The dry heat was about the only thing Pharaoh didn't miss about Phoenix. His white-T clung to his back from the instant sweat, as he exited the terminal. He flagged a yellow cab pulling into the entrance area.

"Migo, can you please take me to the Double Tree Hotel," Pharaoh said handing the Mexican driver a fifty dollar bill. The old man raised the bill into the sun to check its authenticity before starting the meter. Pharaoh sunk low

into the weathered ass printed back seat of the cab. He cracked his window and enjoyed the view of the sky scrapers in downtown Phoenix. The lunch hour traffic sent the meter well over the fifty dollar deposit Pharaoh had given the driver. He passed the driver another fifty as they pulled into the valet of the Double Tree Hotel. Pharaoh climbed out the cab and tapped its trunk as to say thank you. He stepped inside the rotating glass doors behind a middle-aged white woman. He inched his way through the door and into the lobby, where he walked over to the front desk.
"Reservations?" the man working behind the desk asked.
"Yes. Travis Hunt" Pharaoh said providing his alias. He waited while the man verified the reservations.
The man reached inside the drawer beneath his waist and handed Pharaoh a room key-card. "Enjoy your stay," he told him.

Pharaoh took the elevator up to the eleventh floor. When he stepped off the elevator he was standing dead center in a plush presidential suite. He smiled, as he flashed back to his bachelor party going down in the very same suite. Pharaoh set his carry-on luggage on the snow white sectional sofa and reached for the phone. He called the front desk and told them to arrange a concierge service.
"I'll be ready in twenty minutes, and thank you." Pharaoh hung up the phone, and walked into the master bath adjacent to the bedroom. He started a cool shower. While the water was running, Pharaoh raided the mini fridge for a miniature bottle of Moet. He downed the ice cold champagne, and began stripping his clothing on the way back to the shower.

Pharaoh dried off and got dressed. Twenty two minutes had passed, and he was running late. He grabbed two hands full of cash from his carry-on bag and stuffed the bag under the sofa. He grabbed the room key off the glass table near the private elevator and pressed the button for the shaft. Pharaoh stepped through the lobby on his way toward the front desk, the man who had waited on him earlier waved his hand for the young white boy seated in the lobby. Pharaoh met eyes with the young man and changed his stride for the man's direction.

"I'm Jason. I'll be your driver for the night," the young man said, extending his hand for Pharaoh's.

"A'ight," Pharaoh nodded while shaking the driver's hand. They stared for the door.

"So, where'd you like me to take you?" asked Jason.

Are you familiar with the Zone?" Pharaoh asked, while standing at the rear of the black Lincoln Towne car.

Jason opened Pharaoh's door. From the look on his face, he was trying to jog his memory. He walked around the front of the car still thinking.

"Isn't that a bar & grill?" asked Jason, as he shut the driver's door.

"Yeah."

"I know where it's at. I took my girlfriend there a while back." Jason started the engine, checked his mirrors before pulling away from the curb.

Pharaoh couldn't help but ask, "Were there any women working at the Zone, you know like Mexican women?"

Pharaoh sat at the edge of his seat. He knew that Jason could only be talking about one person. Those same beautiful eyes had caused him to lose of breath years back. He couldn't help but wonder if she still looked the same. He fought the urge to ask Jason, he decided to save that surprise for his own eyes.

"You want me to wait for you, or are you going to call the service when you're ready?" Jason asked pulling into the parking lot of the Zone.

"I think you'd better wait. But if I decide to stay, I'll send someone out." Pharaoh tipped Jason and reached for the door handle.

His guts were bubbling as he started for the front entrance of the Zone. Pharaoh stopped before opening the door and took a deep breath. He pulled the handle open to the glass door and stepped inside the cool air conditioned place. Pharaoh really didn't know what to expect from those he was visiting. It had been years since their last communication, and both were victims of betrayal.

"What can I get you?" a barmaid asked, as Pharaoh slid onto a bar stool. The woman was a petite Mexican with long brown hair and had a bright smile.

Pharaoh looked her over and wondered if she was related to the owner. "I'll have a double shot of Remy Martin."

The barmaid smiled and went to fix Pharaoh's drink. He looked around the club, fixating his probe on the office behind the bar. The barmaid answered a male's voice coming from the office "Yes, Papi," she said, setting the glass of Remy Martin in front of Pharaoh.

"I'll be back to check on you," she said.

"Hold on for one second, I want to ask you something," Pharaoh took a sip from his glass then continued. "Does Toro still own the place?"

"Yes, He's in the back. Why'd you want to see him?"

Pharaoh stared blankly. He downed his glass, then said, "Yeah."

"And who should I say is here?"

"Just tell em' it's his son-in-law."

The barmaid frowned in confusion. She said, "Okay," and then turned on her heels. She said something in Spanish as she entered the back office. "Si," she said, pointing Pharaoh out to the old man at her side.

Pharaoh stood to his feet and watched as Toro, his father-in-law, inched down the bar. Toro's face showed no emotion. And Pharaoh was starting to ask himself why he'd dug up the old bones to begin with. Toro walked around the bar and opened up his arms for a hug. His still face pulled back into a huge smile.

"Pharaoh," said Toro, as if he were happy to see him.

Pharaoh reached down and hugged Toro. Their embrace ended with Toro tapping Pharaoh's back. Pharaoh stood back and looked at Toro. He was still speechless, but knew he ought to state his reason for coming. Toro seemed not to harbor any ill feelings, and why should he? It was Valdez who brought down the family. Not Pharaoh.

"Papi," Pharaoh began, "I have come to clear something up."

Toro stuck his hand out interrupting Pharaoh. Toro waved for a table, and they sat. In Toro's tradition it was rude to speak when standing, especially about family.

"As you were saying," said Toro.

"The way things went down, Papi, was inexcusable. But as you know, I had absolutely no part in the snitching that went on. I wanted to make sure that we're alright."

"Son, and I say that because you are still married to my daughter, I never had any discomfort in my heart for you. I know what happened, who ratted and who didn't. You are a man's man, Pharaoh. And I do commend you for not sacrificing your morals and principles. Now, whatever's going on between you and Sasha is out of my control. You know, I wish you two would work things out. But again, I am going to leave that up to you kids. Enough about that. When did you get out?"

"A few weeks ago. I had some things to clean up before I started trial. How about you, what's the status on your case?"

"I too had to clean some things up. Valdez's been missing for almost six months now. The judge cut me loose on a half-million dollar bond so that I could have surgery on my shoulder."

"What about Joey?"

"They're holding onto my boy. They're still digging for fool's gold," laughed Toro. But he should be home soon."

"Good. That's the way it's supposed to be. The bad guys can't always lose."

Toro laughed, and then slapped Pharaoh on his shoulder. "Now, I'll drink to that," he said.

"Maria, bring us a bottle of Cristal," Toro instructed the barmaid.

Pharaoh looked down at the table as he played with one of the brown coasters. His mind had drifted off to the real reason he was there. "Sasha?" Pharaoh said as if it were a question. He looked up at Toro.

"She misses you. She hasn't said it, but I know my daughter. Sasha's still in love with you. Thank you," Toro said taking the Cristal from the barmaid. He poured Pharaoh a glass and then one for himself.

"So, she's not seeing anyone?"

"Hasn't since you left. Come on, let's toast," Toro said waiting for Pharaoh to raise his glass. "Here's to honor and loyalty. For nothing else matters," said Toro.

Pharaoh touched glasses with Toro before taking a sip of the bubbly.

"Don't look so down, son. I tell you what. After we finish our bottle, we'll drive by the house. I'm pretty sure Sasha's there. She was helping her mom with dinner."

"You think she'll want to see me?" asked Pharaoh. He was getting nervous all over again.

"You haven't been listening to a word I've been saying, have you? She hasn't stopped loving you. Of course, she'll be more than happy to see you. Where are you staying?"

"I have a suite at the Double Tree."

"Not anymore. I can't have you staying in some hotel. You can stay at the house." Toro insisted, and Pharaoh knew better than to argue with ole' Toro, he was still clearly in charge.

Pharaoh nodded in agreement.

"Let's have another glass, and then we can go."

Pharaoh waved the barmaid over and asked her to please tell his driver to go on. Pharaoh couldn't hope but wish that ole' Toro really wasn't harboring any ill feelings toward him. If he were, there wouldn't be much Pharaoh could do once they reached the house. Pharaoh drank from his glass while eyeing the old man carefully.

Chapter Nineteen

Pharaoh drummed his fingers nervously on his lap as Toro pulled the black Rolls Royce through the private gates of his Tuscan estate. The house was as beautiful as the first time Pharaoh had been there when Sasha introduced him to her family. Pharaoh scanned the cars looking for Sasha's Lexus, but didn't see it.

"Home sweet, home," said Toro. He parked next to his white Bentley Azure.

Pharaoh got out the car and waited for Toro to walk around his side. Together they walked up the side stone staircase leading to the front doors. Without inserting any keys, Toro pulled the gold-plated lever and pushed open the gigantic wooden door. Pharaoh stepped inside first. The brisk air conditioning replaced the scorching heat that they had experience on the way in.

"Come on. They're probably in the kitchen," said Toro.

Pharaoh, followed close behind Toro as they walked the marble floors through the hall, to the formal dining area, and into the gourmet kitchen. Pharaoh stopped adjacent of the entrance. His eyes fixated on the woman he'd fallen in love with and eventually married. Toro walked around the island where his wife stood preparing salad. He kissed her nape, and said something in Spanish, to which the woman smiled and returned his kisses.

"Papi, did you bring the sauces, like I asked?" asked Sasha. She still had her back to the group, while she rinsed vegetables at the sink.

"No.   But I've brought you something even better," said Toro.   He and his wife watched the scene, both smiling widely as Sasha turned from the sink.

"But Papi, we need…" Sasha's words faded softly as she locked eyes on Pharaoh.   Speechless, she slowly wiped he hands on her apron, and started towards Pharaoh.

Toro said something to his wife, and they both excused themselves from the kitchen.   Sasha's mom gave Pharaoh a slight hug on her way out.   It seemed as if everyone was happy to see him, except Sasha.   He couldn't tell from her body language what she was thinking.

Pharaoh tried to pull back a smile as Sasha neared him, but she cocked back and slapped his face.   There was an awkward silence after that.   Pharaoh's face was slightly stinging, but the slap felt more like love than hate.

"You bastard!   How could you come here?" snared Sasha.   Her breathing had become heavy.   She stared Pharaoh down, her eyes not blinking and demanding an answer.

"Mami," Pharaoh began.   He reached for Sasha, but she refused him.   She took a step back and folded her arms.

"You have a lot of nerve coming here after all you put me and my family through.   What do you want?" asked Sasha, sharply.

"I need to see you.   I needed to see you face to face and apologize for all that happened, I mean between us."

"Well, I don't accept your apology," Sasha said, cutting Pharaoh off.

"And you don't have to.   Coming out here, I never expected you to.   I never expected anything.   Like I said, I, me, I needed to see you and apologize.   What I did was beyond wrong, and there's no way to try to rationalize it. It was wrong, Sasha. And I'm sorry," Pharaoh said sincerely.

"Pharaoh, you brought that boy into our home. You told me he was your nephew, when he was really your son. Do you know how that made me feel, do you have any idea? I fell in love with that little boy."

"I know," Pharaoh said, dropping his eyes to the floor.

"I could have forgiven all the infidelity and whatever else that were going on, but that I cannot forgive this."

"Sasha, when I brought my son home to us, I wanted so bad to tell you and hope that you'd accept it for what it was. I wanted so badly for us to keep him, and raise him in our home, but I couldn't do it. I couldn't keep him from his mom."

"So, you lied to me. Pharaoh, you don't see, we we're living a lie. That's what hurt me. The fact that we were living a lie…"

Pharaoh hadn't gotten the closure he had come for, but it was enough. He could see that his being there was causing Sasha pain. "Maybe, I should go. You continue to take care of yourself," said Pharaoh. He turned to leave, and as he was walking out the kitchen, Sasha said,

"You can at least stay for dinner."

Pharaoh turned back to face Sasha. "You sure?" he asked.

"Yes. Help me set the table," said Sasha.

Pharaoh stepped over to the sink and washed his hands. He could see Toro peaking through the living room doorway. He was smiling giving Pharaoh thumbs up. Pharaoh nodded and smiled.

Toro and his wife walked back into the kitchen, Toro clearing his throat as to announce their presence.

"Papi, what time is everyone expected to be here?" asked Sasha.

Toro looked at his platinum Rolex. "They should be here any moment."

"You kids make up?" asked Sasha's mom. She too, loved Pharaoh and she wanted to see them back together.

"Mami," said Sasha, then she said something else in Spanish.

"He's your husband still," Mom's said waving Sasha off, as she pulled a pan from the oven.

Toro intervened, telling his wife in Spanish to stay out of it. He walked over to the dinner table where Pharaoh stood leaned over placing knife, fork spoon onto napkins beside the spread of plates. Toro took his seat at the head of the table. He lit a cigar and pulled a seat out for Pharaoh.

"Take a seat, son. Let the women take care of that," he ordered.

Pharaoh caught Sasha's under-stare from the stove as he took a seat.

"Finish telling me about your end of things," said Toro.

"What do you mean?" asked Pharaoh.

"The conspiracy," Toro said in a low-tone.

"As of right now, I'm still on the run. I kinda escaped from the County jail, and while I was out I used that time to clean things up."

"When are you going to put this all behind you?"

"Soon as I get back to Detroit I'm going to turn myself in, and then we can have a trial, but without all those witnesses."

"Well, just as soon as all this is over. We can resume in our operation. You know, you'll always have a spot. Maybe you can take over Valdez's spot."

Pharaoh looked over at Sasha. He didn't want to commit himself to another run just yet. "We'll see, Papi," said Pharaoh.

Sasha and her mom sat the spread of food at the center of the table, and went back into the kitchen to grab all the side dishes. Within minutes, the house came alive. Sasha's family showed up in numbers. They all greeted each other in Spanish, hugging Toro at the neck and kissing his forehead. Ambria, Sasha's sister, met eyes with Pharaoh. She turned to Sasha and asked. "What is he doing here?" Toro became angry. He slammed his hands down hard on the table making the plates and silverware jump. He looked at this daughter Ambria and scolded her. He said: "It was your ratona, husband, Valdez who tried to bring this family down. Not my son, Pharaoh. So, I want nothing but respect to be shown to him. Do I make myself clear?"

"Yes, Papi," Ambria said almost in a whisper.

Toro looked around the kitchen at the rest of them with a look on his face that said, "That goes for all of you." Even with Toro coming to his rescue, Pharaoh was still uncomfortable. He ate very little during dinner, but didn't excuse himself from the table until pretty much everyone moved outside to the pool area. He didn't want to be rude.

Pharaoh had been seated next to Sasha at the dinner table. An awkward silence lingered between them.

"Let me help you with these," Pharaoh said, helping Sasha clear the table of dishes.

"I'll take care of the dishes. You kids go enjoy yourselves." Mom shooed, Pharaoh and Sasha out the kitchen.

'I really don't feel like going out there," Pharaoh said looking out the patio door at Sasha's family. They were all gathered around the pool.

"Well, let's take a walk. We need to talk some more," said Sasha. She led the way out the front door.

Pharaoh tucked both his hands into his pants pocket and walked with his head to the ground, as he tried to think of something meaningful to say. "Sasha, do you feel like what I did is beyond forgiveness?"

"I never thought about it like that. I guess I sorta knew that we'd eventually see each other again. But as far as forgiving you, the damage is done, Pharaoh."

Pharaoh stopped under a huge Oak tree in front of an estate, three properties down from Toro's. He picked his head up from the ground and stared deep into Sasha's green eyes.

"Sasha, you are still my wife, and I'm still your husband. And there's a reason why we're still married. Not because we just hadn't gotten around to getting a divorce. It's been years. I know the damage is done. But what I need from you, so that we both can move on is whether or not the damage can be fixed? Did you ever stop loving me? I mean, I see you're still wearing your ring…" Pharaoh reached for Sasha's hand. He rubbed the back of her hand using his thumb, while looking for an answer in her eyes.

"I never said that I stopped loving you, Pharaoh," Sasha said looking away. She took a step up the sidewalk, and together they continued…

"I'll always love you. But I'm fighting with can I ever trust you again. That will always be in the back of my mind."

"Sasha, it would be unrealistic for me to think any different. Of course, you'll always remember, but what I need is your forgiveness. That was something that should have never happened, but it did and I regret it every day, because that is what's been keeping us apart. I need for you to forgive me, so I can forgive myself for messing up our happy home."

"I forgive you, Papi."

Pharaoh hadn't let go of Sasha's hand. He stopped and pulled her close to him. "Thank you," he said looking into her welling eyes. Pharaoh wiped two streaming tears from Sasha's face. "Mami, don't cry," he softly pleaded. "It's going to be alright."

"Okay," Sasha sniffled.

Pharaoh looked up over Sasha's shoulder and his eyes widened like he was staring at a pot of gold. "Is that our…" he cut his question short, as Sasha turned around to face the mansion.

"Yes, that's our home," Sasha said, gripping Pharaoh's hand. "Come on, she said pulling him along.

Toro had bought the estate as a wedding gift when Pharaoh and Sasha first got married. The estate was only a few houses away from Sasha's parents.

"You've stayed here all this time?" asked Pharaoh, as he and Sasha entered the front door.

"Yes. It is our home, remember?" Sasha locked the door and tossed her keys on the small stand in the hall. "You're acting like you've never been here before. Come on in and relax," Sasha said heading into the living room.

"It's not that," Pharaoh said looking around the mansion, "It's just hard to believe that I once lived here." Pharaoh sunk into the beige Italian leather sofa.

Sasha smiled and said, "I'll be right back."

Pharaoh reached for the remote on the lamp post. He kicked his shoes off and wrapped his arms around the back of the sofa while flicking through the channels. Sasha returned carrying two champagne glasses and a bottle of Moet. She popped the cork and poured two glasses.

"Here," she said handing one to Pharaoh.

"What are we toasting to?"

"Nothing. This will just help take the edge off," said Sasha. She unfastened her Stiletto's and set them at the corner of the sofa. She grabbed her glass and took a seat close to Pharaoh, tucking her legs underneath her sundress.

"What do you want to watch?" asked Pharaoh.

"You," Sasha said facing Pharaoh.

He sat the remote down and took a long sip from his glass, before setting it down as well.

"You've grown a lot," said Sasha.

"What do you mean?"

"Mustache and beard has thickened, and your voice is a lot deeper. Your forehead has lines that weren't there before." Sasha was looking Pharaoh over.

"From stressing."

"Yeah."

"But what about you?" Pharaoh examined Sasha's face. She was as beautiful as the day he first met her at the Zone. "Where does your stress go? You're still that same beautiful woman I fell in love with three years ago."

Sasha blushed, and then dropped her head. Pharaoh raised her chin with his index finger, and they locked eyes. Pharaoh wrapped Sasha's long black hair around her ear, gracefully laying its ends over her shoulder. The way he used to do it.

"I still love you." Not waiting for Sasha to respond, Pharaoh leaned into Sasha's lips. He didn't attempt to kiss her just yet, he allowed their lips to barely touch, as he enjoyed her scent and breathing over his face. Sasha didn't refuse him. She closed her eyes and raised her hand to the back of Pharaoh's hand, which he used to hold the side of her face.

"I love you," whispered Pharaoh before he began kissing around Sasha's mouth.

Pharaoh ended the barrage of affectionate pecks, and pulled Sasha close to his chest.

Together they stretched out the long way across the sofa, with Sasha lying halfway on top of Pharaoh. She rested one hand in the center of his chest, while looking up at him.

Pharaoh reached for the remote and turned off the TV, then clicked the stereo system on. He let his hands ride slowly up the back of Sasha's thighs, up to her back, where they rested. Luther Vandross helped set the mood. "Knowing love the way I do. I can say for certain that it's true. There's a chance for me and you..." Those few lyrics had summed it all up. That's exactly what Pharaoh wanted to say but couldn't find the words. He decided to let Luther do the talking, while he gave Sasha something he had never given a woman in his life, his heart.

Pharaoh just lay back and ran his fingers through Sasha's hair, while they forgave each other's absence through a powerful stare.

"I remember spending all my time. On a dream that kept me wishing... That you could be mine...."

Chapter Twenty

Two weeks had passed, and Pharaoh spent every minute of them trying to repair his marriage. He and Sasha were inseparable, just like they were before Pharaoh went to jail and the feds revealed his secret life to Sasha.

Pharaoh was stretched out across the plush mattress of their king sized bed with his back exposed to the ceiling. He lay there with a towel wrapped around his waist and his face buried into two throw pillows. Sasha squirted Jergens lotion on his back and began rubbing it deep into his pores, mixing in the small beads of shower water which remained at the shoulder of Pharaoh. Sasha worked her hands in firm circles. "Aaaah," Pharaoh sighed from the pillows. It felt so good, that he thought for a second he was at a massage parlor.

Pharaoh was dreading what lied ahead of him for the day. But it was time…

"Roll over, Papi."

Pharaoh rolled onto his back and covered his face with one of the pillows. He felt the cool Jergens lotion splat onto his chest, and Sasha's soft hands starting at his shoulder blades. She rubbed lotion onto both Pharaoh's arms down to his hands and in between his fingers. He felt the towel come loose and lotion being rubbed between his thighs and down his legs. By the time Sasha worked her way up, Pharaoh was standing at attention. Sasha looked at Pharaoh, who was still buried under the pillow. She squeezed some lotion on her right hand and softly gripped

Pharaoh's dick. She watched as Pharaoh's body slightly shivered from her soft stroke. She jacked him off until he was about to bust, then rolled up her long T-shirt to her waist. Sasha climbed on top of Pharaoh. She held his dick, while guiding him inside her.

Sasha closed her eyes as she slid down Pharaoh's manhood. She moaned softly after burying Pharaoh deep inside her. She placed both of her hands on Pharaoh's chest, using them as support to ride out. Sasha scrubbed her soft ass against Pharaoh's pelvis, making her walls contact with every thrust. "Oh, Papi. Ah," She moaned picking up the pace. Pharaoh couldn't stand another thrust. He began skeeting at the sound of Sasha's soft voice.

"Papi.." Sasha whispered, as she joined Pharaoh in ecstasy. She rode him until he went limp, then pulled the pillow from his face and started kissing him all over. "I wish you didn't have… to go," Sasha said between each kiss.

"Me too, Mami."

"Let's just wait until the day they catch you. Why must you turn yourself in?" Sasha sat up. She rubbed her juices around Pharaoh's soft dick.

"It's the best thing to do. Besides, I promised my friend I'd take care of things. He probably thinks I left him hanging."

"I understand."

"I knew you would. That's why I love you."

Sasha leaned down and gave Pharaoh a long wet passionate kiss. She pulled up and looked Pharaoh in his eyes.

"Hurry back, Papi."

"I will," promised Pharaoh.

"Pharaoh, are you ready?   The plane leaves in twenty minutes," Yelled Toro.

"I gotta get going."   Pharaoh gave Sasha a peck beforeshe rolled off him.

She watched as he dressed.   Sasha didn't want to see him leave because she feared something might happen to cause him not to return.

"You sure you don't want to ride with us to the airport?" asked Pharaoh, buttoning his shirt.   He bent down to tie his shoes.   "You hear me, Mami?"

"No. It'll hurt me too much to watch you leave on a plane."

"Sasha, I promise that'll I will be back."

Sasha closed her eyes, while Pharaoh kissed the top of her head and rubbed the side of her face.   When she opened her eyes, Pharaoh was gone.   She fell back into the comfort of the pillows and stared up at the ceiling...

"Sasha's not coming?"   Toro asked, as Pharaoh reached the bottom step.

"She doesn't want to see me leave."

"How sweet," teased Toro.   "We better get moving, or you're going to miss your flight."

Pharaoh took one long look at the mansion from the passenger seat of Toro's Bentley.   'I promise,' he thought, as Toro pulled out the driveway.

Toro pushed the Bentley down I-75 doing 85 mph, but the smoothness of the ride only felt like they were doing 30 mph.   Pharaoh was slouched in his seat looking out the window.

"You've got ten minutes," Toro said checking his Rolex. He pulled up to the entrance and flipped the hazards on.

"Come on." Toro pulled on the door handle and walked around to Pharaoh's side.

Pharaoh reluctantly climbed out the car and shut the door. Toro extended his hand for Pharaoh's but pulled him close for a hug. The old man wrapped his small hands around Pharaoh's back and patted him twice.

"I'll be here when you get back. Go on and take care of business, son."

Pharaoh could hear the love in Toro's voice. He rubbed the top of the old man's graying head and nodded with a smile.

"Go on," said Toro.

Pharaoh stepped through the automated sliding doors into the terminal. His flight number had just come across the crackling intercom. "All passengers, please board the plane."

Pharaoh stepped to the wooden podium where an attendant checked him in for the flight. The heavy set middle-aged sista looked over the rim of her glasses at Pharaoh's ticket, and then nodded him on. Pharaoh took a window seat in first-class. He fastened his seatbelt, then reclined his chair and closed his eyes. "Thank you," he said in a whisper.

Chapter Twenty One

It was 4:30 a.m. and Ollie had yet to get some sleep. He sat on the edge of his bed with his feet dangling over the side. He nervously swung his legs back and forth under the steel frame of the bed. "I can't believe you played me," he said as if someone was standing before him. Ollie reached under his thin mattress and felt around for an envelope. He grabbed the tip of the envelope and pulled it from under the mattress. He pulled its content from the sleeve. He read the letter a hundred times, reading it once more wouldn't hurt things any.

Dear Ollie:

My dude, I know you're thinking that I done forgot about you and I could see why. But know that what we discussed is on the grill and is almost done...

Ollie bald the letter up and threw it in the toilet. He watched the ink from blue lines on the paper bleed and changed the color of the water. He was angry because Pharaoh hadn't done one thing he said he would. And worse, the government moved his trial date up. He was scheduled to have an evidentiary hearing today to determine whether the government had enough evidence to proceed with a trial.

Ollie had been walking with his head down. "Today's the day, huh?" Ollie asked raising his head to Klip and Tuck.

"Yeah..." Tuck dragged, as they stepped on the elevator.

"Damn, old head. You stressin' 'bout something. What's up?" Klip asked. He was unfazed by his own fate. He'd been to trial several times before and had beaten murder beefs, so today was no different.

"Ain't nothing. Nothing I can't fix," Ollie responded. The battered elevator stopped on the ground floor of the annex building. The two sheriffs stepped off the shaft first. The busted-body white sheriff wiped sweat from his forehead and pushed his sliding bifocals up on his nose. "I'ma hold up the rear," he told the young black sheriff who led the group down a flight of stone slab steps and through the underground tunnel over to Registry, where the group climbed another flight of steps back up to the ground floor.
Reaching the automated door of Registry, Ollie gave Klip and Tuck some dap. "Good luck," he wished them both.
"You too, O.G," Tuck said as they all went their separate ways. The deputy working the booth cracked holding pen #2 for Ollie. Pen #2 is where they held all the federal prisoners.

Ollie scanned the filthy cell and opted to stand, because pissy tissue scattered across the floor and empty cereal bowls and milk cartons decorated the small steel benches. Ollie stood close to the bars and watched the many faces being ushered to the assorted bullpens. The lights in Registry came on at about 7:30 a.m. and the deputies began finger printing each holding tank. After getting their print taken, each prisoner was handed his morning breakfast, consisting of one milk, pastry, carton of orange juice and two small bowls of Trix cereal.

Ollie waved the deputy no, declining his breakfast on his way back to the pen. The uncertainty of his fate had Ollie on pins and needles. Every time he thought about Pharaoh, he became angry. 'I was the only nigga who kept it real. And this is how you gone play me?' Ollie thought. He paced the dirt smeared floor of the cell with his hands behind his back. The clock posted on the wall inside the Registry booth read 8:20 a.m. Two U.S. Marshals appeared in front of the holding tank. The 30- something crew-cut wearing black Marshal set a steel case on the ledge of the booth and popped its latch open. He began pulling belly chains and ankle bracelets from the box and setting them on the floor in front of Ollie's cell.

The silver haired husky white Marshal pulled a piece of paper from the slot on the booth and began reading name off. Ollie along with seven others were lined up outside the bullpen and searched, then chained up at the wrist and ankle. The group was ushered through the sliding door and into the parking garage. They scooted toward the silver fifteen passenger van, where crew-cut placed a stool at the double doors for the prisoners to climb inside.

Ollie was last to get in the van. He reached down and adjusted the ankle cuffs because they were biting into his shins. Ollie's last court date had been over a year ago. The morning sun nearly blinded him as he leaned against the cage window. His eyes widened at the sight of freedom. The van tucked from under the county's garage and made a wide right on Beaubien Street. Smog from a manhole engulfed the windshield and spread across the side window. The smog seemed to resemble Ollie's mood. For some reason, he felt like that would be the last ride through the city. His next one would be to the penitentiary.

The van slowed as it neared the corner of Lafayette. The Marshal dipped into the underground tunnel beneath the Federal Courthouse. The van stopped in front of the control booth and the two Marshals began grabbing the belly chains and assorted documents from the space between them. The entire van and tunnel was dead still. The only thing which could be heard was the Marshal's pulling on the door handles. They said something to the white man standing on the landing of the control center. The man plucked his half smoked cigarette and nodded to the Marshals. Crew-cut, opened the side doors and placed the stool down. Ollie turned sideways and inched out the van. He had to clinch his teeth from cussing, as he stepped down on the stool as the ankle cuffs dug deep into his skin. He inched up the ramp to the elevator where the second Marshal stood.

"Get on the elevator. Face to the wall," ordered the silver haired vet.

They packed the shaft, and then took it up to the sixth floor. There was a Marshal waiting on the other side of the elevator door when the shaft reached the sixth floor. He read names from a white sheet of paper that was marked with yellow and pink highlighters. Ollie was pointed to an attorney visiting booth. His anklets and belly-chain were removed and he adjusted his county green outfit on his way to the booth.

"Have a seat," his lawyer said without looking up from the stacks of papers in front of him.

Ollie paced the small floor instead. "Well," Ollie said impatiently.

Mr. Dunlap removed his stretched out reading glasses from his fat face, then folded them. He slid them into their sleek case, and stuffed all the papers he'd been pretending to read into a manila folding envelope. He sat the glass case dead center of the envelope nice and neat, then finally focused on Ollie. "I suggest you consider cooperating with the government. That is, if you ever want to see the streets again."

Ollie slammed his yellow hand against the thick coiled gate between them. He peered into Mr. Dunlap's blue eyes. "Listen, you fat bastard. I done told you about insulting me with all these rat propositions."

"But I was just looking…"

Ollie cut him short. "What you need to be doing is figuring out a strategy for when we get in this court room. How you get me from under this shit!"

"I did not mean to upset you. We're clear on the direction we're moving in."

"We damn sure betta be. Cause if I get sold out in there, I'm telling you…"

"Understood," Mr. Dunlap said sliding back in his chair. He stood up and grabbed his folder and glasses. "I'll see you upstairs. I believe you're scheduled for 1:00 p.m."

Ollie glared at his lawyer as he stepped out the visiting booth. 'Mothafucka, sorry white-bitch!' Ollie cursed to himself. He paced the floor with his hands crossed behind his back until the Marshal waved him out. He walked down a short gated hallway and waited at pen #4 until the Marshal buzzed him in. Ollie nodded at the African man to his right and two Chinese men seated on the floor Indian-style. He took a seat on the empty bench and did as the other men were doing, waited.

Ollie thought back to every possible event of him, Tez and Pharaoh; from grade school, to sitting in the spot, to robbing the bank and going to jail, to coming home to more money he'd ever seen in his short-life. But it was just that, short-lived. 'If I don't beat this shit, I'ma be just another young dumb nigga lost in the system,' Ollie thought. He got to thinking about all the things he'd done, and all the things he hadn't. The side of the "had nots" were weighing heavy on his scale. It's called regret.

Ollie stood and went over to the sink. He splashed cold water on his face, then stared himself in the face through the polished mirror mounted above the sink/toilet. 'It is what it is,' he told himself. He used a wad of toilet paper to blot his face dry. He flushed the tissue, and kicked back on the bench with his eyes locked on the ceiling. The Marshals wheeled two trays down the hallway and handed each man his lunch due, a club sandwich, Better-made plain potato chips, and a small Styrofoam cup of flat cola.

As soon as Ollie set his spread beside him, the door clicked and the Marshal yelled from the end of the hall for him to hurry up, he had court in five minutes.

"I'm ready now!" Ollie yelled stepping to the gate door. He put his fingers through the holes on the gate and waited for a response. The gate clicked once more and Ollie pulled it open. He nodded to the African, then at his food, offering it to him. "Thank you" The African said to Ollie as he started down the hall. A short slender young faced white Marshal ushered Ollie and two other men onto an awaiting elevator. "Face to wall," The Marshal said sharply before pushing their floor button.

The shaft stopped on the fourth floor and Ollie was escorted off by two court Marshals. They led him to Judge Hathaway's courtroom. The tall man-build female Marshal pointed for the defense table as if Ollie didn't know where his seat was. Ollie was stuntin' ole' bull-dagger. His heart sunk as what he feared, was a reality. With the exception of the prosecution, a few agents, Ollie's lawyer and the two Marshals, the courtroom was empty. It seemed everyone was there to put him away, including Ollie's own attorney. His only focus was converting Ollie into a full blown rat.

Ollie sunk into the leather seat beside Mr. Dunlap. The feds were something else. They wanted you to at least be comfortable when they served your fate. Ollie laid his head back against the tall head rest. The clerk entered the courtroom with Judge Hathaway on her heels.

"All rise…" Judge Hathaway sighed as he settled onto his throne. The young fifty-something white man rolled back his sleeves to his robe and brushed his full head of hair to the back with both hands. He did a quick drum on the desk before him and then said "Okay- we're here for an evidentiary hearing?"

"That is correct," U.S. Assistant Attorney, Francis Carlson stood and said.

"Very well. Would you like to please present the government's case, as it would in trial," Hathaway said sitting back in his chair and folding his arms.

"Well, your honor. The government intends to prove at trial the defendants involvement in the extensive marijuana conspiracy that rooted in Arizona, and extended back to Detroit."

"What evidence does the government intend on introducing at trial?" asked Hathaway.

"Unexplained wealth' receipts and various paraphernalia to support the defendants unexplainable lavish life-style."

"What about corroborating evidence, will the court hear any testimony from persons defendant supposedly purchased these items from?"

"Your honor, the defendant is a very dangerous man. As you may be aware, his co-defendant is on the run right now after escaping from the Wayne County Jail."

"Yes, I am aware. But please answer my question. Does the government have any witnesses scheduled to testify?"

"Your honor, all the witnesses in this case mysteriously either disappeared, or were found shot to death."

"So, the answer to my question is no."

"Your honor, if I may," Mr. Dunlap said standing and walking over to the podium. He adjusted the mic on its coiled rod to level his stature. "Your honor, I understand that it's the government's prerequisite not to reveal its strategies of trial, and even some evidence. However, what we're trying to established here, is what witnesses will be testifying. Then and only then, can we determine whether sufficient evidence exist to warrant a trial.

"I understand," said Hathaway.

"What I am asking, is for the government to advise the court what witnesses in particular are missing and who's dead?

Because if I'm not mistaken, there was only one witness who's testimony involved my client in the conspiracy. The rest were as Ms. Carlson said, witnesses about unexplained wealth. If that's the case, we need to be having a trial on tax invasion, not conspiracy."

"Ms. Carlson," Judge Hathaway said turning his attention on the circle-faced Chinese woman.

Ms. Carlson was obviously distraught and pissed at the same time. She had to give Ollie the news he'd been waiting to hear.

"Your honor, I am afraid that the key witness in this investigation was killed at his apartment weeks ago."

Ollie damn near jumped out of his seat. He took a deep breath, as Mr. Dunlap put his hand on his leg and pinched him. Ollie fought back a smile. He turned slightly in his chair looking into the back of the courtroom. The smile won the fight, as it spread wide across Ollie's face. He was staring his best friend in the face. Pharaoh winked at Ollie and formed his mouth into a closed grin.

Ollie's ears turned back into the babbling of Ms. Carlson. "...undoubtedly his co-defendant is responsible for these brutal murders."

"Your honor," Mr. Dunlap dragged his words to silence Ms. Carlson. He continued after standing. This is all speculation. And has nothing to do with my client."

"It has everything to do with him. I am asking the court not to release this man. He is a danger to the general public."

"Your honor, based on the government's own omissions of lack of evidence, I am now moving for a dismissal. A trial would only be a waste of time, government tax-dollars, and energy."

"I'll be the one to determine such. Court is in recess till further notice..." Hathaway rose and dismissed himself into his chambers.

Chapter Twenty Two

After a thirty-five minute recess, Judge Hathaway emerged from his chambers. The clerk announced his entry as before. Rolling up his sleeves, brushing his hair back and a quick drum on the scattered desk, he proceeded, "This is the part of the law that I hate, and intend to fix one day when I'm serving as Supreme Court Justice. It is truly one of the many glitches in the justice system where the wheels of justice allows criminals such as yourself to slip through the cracks and back out into society. I am reluctant to set you free, but under the law, I must. There lacks sufficient evidence to support cause of a trial. So, I am hereby ordering dismissal of all charges without prejudice."

Ollie hugged, Mr. Dunlap at the neck and patted his back. Pharaoh stood to his feet and slid out from between the benches. He walked up to Ollie and reached over the small wooden railing between them. He gave Ollie a tight hug. They ended their embrace by hitting rocks.

Pharaoh gave Mr. Dunlap the keys to his 500 "SL and said, "Make sure he gets them once he's released."

Ollie's smile dwindled… "What you 'bout to do, P?" he asked, fearing the answer.

"It's time I put my running behind me." Pharaoh hugged Ollie once more, before removing his Dob hat from his head. He turned on his heel and slowly walked over to the prosecution table. Ms. Carlson was so pissed from the judge's decision, she hadn't noticed Pharaoh standing there.

She was mumbling something foreign as she stuffed her leather briefcase.

Pharaoh grunted clearing his throat. Ms. Carlson's eyes traveled from the powder-blue gators Pharaoh wore, up his slacks, to his face. She stumbled backward a bit.

Pharaoh pulled back a smile that spelled victory. "Hi! Ms. Carlson. I'm ready to have a trial now," said Pharaoh holding his smile firm.

Ms. Carlson finally caught the words she was fighting to say. "It's him!" she yelled, pointing at Pharaoh. "Arrest him, now!" she ordered.

The two court Marshals rushed to the scene, and asked what seemed to be the problem.

"This is Pharaoh Dickson, defendant number one. He escaped from custody. Arrest him," advised Carlson.

Pharaoh stuck his arms out in anticipation of the cuffs. He hadn't stopped smiling. He knew it would all be behind him soon enough.

"Hold it down, my nigga!" Pharaoh shouted over his shoulder at Ollie, as the Marshals rushed him out the court room.

Chapter Twenty Three

Suited and booted, Pharaoh hit the Wayne County jail in style. He had prepared for the inevitable and was ready to face up, so he could put it all behind him. Due to his escape, Pharaoh was deemed public enemy #1 by the higher-ups. They rushed him through dress-out, putting him in a yellow max security outfit. Five deputies stood by while Pharaoh dressed, and one sergeant for security sake. They handcuffed him behind his back and ushered him through the underground tunnel over to the annex building. The group took the elevator up to the sixth floor. Pharaoh was led down a long hallway and into a max security ward, where cameras sat posted in front of each cell.

The sergeant made sure Pharaoh got the bare minimum as far as toiletries and bedroll. "Baby steps," the short, older man said. He supervised Pharaoh's cell before the convoy turned to leave Pharaoh to his loft.

Pharaoh kicked back on his flat air mattress and took in a deep breath of the county's stench. It hadn't bothered him one bit, because he knew it wouldn't be long before he joined Ollie on the bricks. Pharaoh didn't even bother to make his bed. He just rolled onto his side and pulled one of the lint covered sheets halfway over his body. He closed his eyes and slowly drifted off to sleep.

The following morning Pharaoh was awakened by a sexy familiar voice, "I know you hear me... You ain't sleep."

Pharaoh pulled the sheet from his face and sat up on his elbows. He waited for his eyes to adjust to the fluorescent light beaming into his cell. It was Stacy.

Pharaoh rolled off the bunk and stepped into his shower shoes, then over to the bars. "What's up?" he asked dryly.

"That's all you can say, is what up?" Stacy folded her arms and stared at Pharaoh as he wiped his face into his hands.

"What you want me to say?"

"Something. It's been what, almost three months and you haven't called me. What are they going to do with you?"

"You know what they're trying to do. They tryin' to give me life," said Pharaoh.

"Hmh… Well, it serves you right. How you played, I knew it would come back to haunt you in the end."

"That's what you think, this is the end? Let me tell you something. This ain't my end," Pharaoh said sharp.

"I see you're still living in fantasy land. Well, don't let me interrupt. I'll send you a post card in say, twenty-five years." Stacy dropped her hands and turned on her heels.

"Bitch, fuck you," Pharaoh said to Stacy's back, as she walked off.

Chapter Twenty Four

Mr. Pitts, Pharaoh's attorney, delivered him the news he'd been waiting on for the past four days. They sat in one of the small visiting cells adjacent to the hallway. Pharaoh had his back to the bars and his ears open.

"Judge Hathaway has agreed that there lacks sufficient evidence to grant a trial, but, you know there's always a but…the government wants to try you on escape charges."

"That's the least of my worries. Escape carries what a five year maximum sentence?" asked Pharaoh. He shrugged. "I can do that on my head."

"You may not have to do another day."

"What do you mean?" asked Pharaoh.

"I'm not convinced the government can prove you escaped."

"Ohh.. I like where you're going."

"I mean, really. After reading and re-reading the complaint, it dawned on me they never stated exactly how you escaped. There were no sawed bars, no busted window, identity exchanges with other inmates. Nothing. As far as I'm concerned, they let you go by mistake."

"That's what I've been tryna tell these folks around here," Pharaoh smacked his lips and placed his hands on the small table. He and Mr. Pitts shared in laughter.

"Now all I have to do is convince Judge Hathaway to see it that way. It shouldn't be that hard." said Mr. Pitts.

"And how soon can we be in court?"

"I'm going to try by the end of the week. Ole' Hathaway owes me a few favors. Its' time I cashed one of them in.

Mr. Pitts stood and began gathering his papers. "In the meantime, just do as you've been doing, and sit tight."

Pharaoh patted, Mr. Pitts on the back as he stood. He rung the buzzard for the deputy, and said, "You pull this off and I'ma have to start calling you Lil' Johnny Cochran. And you know what comes with that? Big bonuses."

"I'm on it," Mr. Pitts said as the female deputy opened the gate.

She let Mr. Pitts onto the visitors' elevator, then came back for Pharaoh. He grinned from ear to ear as he stepped into his stride. He had never been so happy to be returning back to a cell. 'Matter of day,' Pharaoh told himself, as the iron gate to his cell slammed behind him.

Chapter Twenty Five

Pharaoh was sitting on the steel table slightly turned toward the television mounted on the bars inside of the black case. His back was to the bars when the call came from the gate.

"Dickson! Roll it up."

Pharaoh turned around and strained his eyes down the long rock freckled faced fat young deputy,

"What court?" asked Pharaoh.

"No… You're being released. I'll be back in five minutes, be ready."

Pharaoh jumped from the table and bolted for the gate, bypassing his cell altogether. There was nothing in there that he couldn't live without. Coming to a sliding stop in his shower shoes, Pharaoh told the light-skinned deputy.

"Man, pull me now before they realize it's a mistake and change their mind." Pharaoh pulled at the bars.

The deputy smiled and said, "I know that's right." He pulled the lever to open the gate.

Pharaoh brushed passed him in a hurry.

"Hold on pimping. Let me lock this up." The deputy caught up to Pharaoh's power-walk. Together, they took the long hall down to the annex elevator.

Stacy was working on the opposite end of the floor. She stood from her chair and opened the gate. Her eyes were fixated on Pharaoh's floor card in the deputy's hand. "Where are you taking him and why isn't he handcuffed?"

Pharaoh pulled back a smile as the young deputy informed Stacy of his immediate release.

"Released?" Stacy repeated.

"Yes… sir," Pharaoh said with as much sarcasm as he could muster.

Stacy snatched, Pharaoh's floor card from the young deputy and imposed her senior officer card. "I'll escort him over to Registry," she said dismissing the man.

Pharaoh stepped onto the elevator and Stacy followed. As soon as the door shut, she was all over Pharaoh trying to kiss his face. Pharaoh refused her altogether. He grabbed her hands and used them to push distance between them.

"Fuck are you doing?" he asked.

"You knew ya' ass wasn't about to do no life. You comin' home to me."

"Imagine that. You right, I did know that I was going to walk. I knew that a long time ago. Back when you kept telling me my ideas were far-fetched. Remember?"

"Pharaoh, what can I say? I was afraid."

"Yeah, afraid to believe in me."

The elevator reached the ground floor and they stepped off. Stacy pleaded her case the entire walk through the tunnel over to Registry. Pharaoh let her pour her little heart out, but as soon as they reached the sliding door of Registry, Pharaoh cut Stacy off and said, "Bottom line is you didn't believe in me, and when you thought that I was washed up, you found comfort elsewhere. We can never be, Stacy. It's over."

Pharaoh left, Stacy standing there with a shitty face. He walked around to the change-out room. The deputy behind the glass remembered Pharaoh coming in earlier that week. He retrieved Pharaoh's clothes and passed them through the window.

Stacy was standing at the corner of the Registry booth when Pharaoh bent the corner of the change-out room. He adjusted his dob to the side of his head, not losing a step. He didn't bother to acknowledge Stacy as he passed her. She reluctantly followed him through the wrap-around hallway leading to the jail's main lobby.

Pharaoh adjusted his powder-blue blazer, and then checked his gators while he waited to be buzzed out. Mr. Pitts identified Pharaoh as his client to the deputy working at the front desk. Pharaoh continued to show Stacy the disdain she earned. He adjusted his shoulders one last time before grabbing the handle of the buzzing door. He could feel the hate piercing through the back of his head from Stacy as he entered the lobby. Mr. Pitts opened his arms for a wide hug.

"I convinced the son-a-bitch to sign your release papers last night," Pitts said ending their embrace.

"I guess, I owe you that bonus. Lil' Johnny," smiled Pharaoh.

"Come on. Let's get the hell out of here," Mr. Pitts said wrapping his arm around Pharaoh's shoulder and leading him out the stainless steel double doors.

"Surprise!"

Pharaoh stopped on the sidewalk and looked at all the faces he loved dearly. Mom Dukes was at the curb with Chyna and Jr., Sasha and Toro were next to Maurice. And Ollie was pulling up in the 500 SL. He got out the car leaving it running in the middle of the street, and stepped around the small crowd. Ollie cocked his hand back for a play, then pulled Pharaoh in for a long hug. They rocked from side to side.

"I love you, my nigga," Ollie spoke into Pharaoh's ear.

"Love you too," said Pharaoh.

When their embrace ended, both men had tears in their eyes. Ollie wiped a tear from his eye before it could fall.

"What we gon' do now?" he asked Pharaoh.

"Enjoy life," said Pharaoh. He reached down for Jr. and picked him up into his arms. "Hey lil' me. You miss daddy?"

"Yeah…"

Sasha joined Pharaoh. She locked her arms into his and gave him a passionate kiss.

Mom Dukes was on her feet and off the respirator. She cried tears of joy to see her son out of jail and with his family. She joined the hug, as did Chyna. Pharaoh raised his head to the sky and mouthed the single word. 'Thank you.'

The End

Epilogue

'Life couldn't have been any more perfect,' thought Pharaoh as he lounged on the back patio of his mansion out in Phoenix with Sasha. They were eating fresh strawberries and sippin' Moet while watching Jr. play in the pool. Sasha was curled up under Pharaoh's arm with her bare feet tucked underneath her. She fed him strawberries while gazing into his eyes.

"What are you smiling about, Papi?"

Pharaoh had the hugest grin on his face. He had every reason in the world to be smiling. Hell, he just beat the feds for one. Tez rat ass was six feet under where he belonged, and he was laid up with one of the most beautiful woman God ever created.

"I'm just so thankful to be here with you. This is where I want to be." Pharaoh gave Sasha a peck on the lips, and then wrapped her long black hair around her ear. "I love you."

"I love you too, Papi."

Pharaoh turned his attention back to the pool. Ollie was tossing Jr. into the water, just having a good ole' time. Everything was perfect. Pharaoh had Jr. living between Phoenix and Detroit. Chyna wasn't tripping on him like she used to. They had set their differences to the side for the sake of Jr. Pharaoh kept his word and bought a building for Chyna to open up her own salon, and he even paid for her to go back to school. Pharaoh's mom was home and out of Rehab. Pharaoh moved her out to Phoenix so she'd be close to him, just to make sure that nothing like that ever happened again. Everything on Pharaoh's list was scratched and checked. All he had to do was kick back and enjoy his money. And that's exactly what he planned to do, despite Toro's generous and tempting offer to head the family business. Toro was an old gangster, he hadn't learned his lesson yet and he wanted to press forward.

Pharaoh turned the offer down, and told him that he was grateful for the opportunity, but he'd have to pass. Pharaoh learned one valuable lesson from the whole situation, and that was to never do business with family or people you love, because there may come a time you've got to kill them, and Pharaoh didn't want to be in that position again.

Ollie, however, wanted to still try his hand at another run in the game. He felt like he never got his time to shine while Pharaoh and Tez were out getting all that money. He had been on lock down. Ollie always caught the bad breaks, but he never folded under pressure. So now, all he wanted was his due shine. He stayed in Pharaoh's ear on how they could make another run, but Pharaoh wasn't going for it.

"I'm going to freshen up the lemonade. You want me to get you anything else, Papi?" Sasha stood at the sight of Ollie climbing out the pool. She wanted to give Pharaoh his privacy.

"I'm okay, baby," said Pharaoh.

Sasha leaned down and gave him a kiss, then slid open the patio door to the kitchen.

Ollie took the seat next to Pharaoh and kicked back. "This is the life, ain't it?" he asked.

"Wouldn't trade it for the world."

"Daddy, look at me," Jr. said from the diving board.

Pharaoh smiled as his son did a cannon ball making a huge splash.

"P, my nigga. I been thinking about what all you said and I feel you. You got too much to lose by getting back in the game. You got your wife, son, big ass mansion, money. I wouldn't give all that up neither. But I need you to feel me. I don't have none of that," said Ollie.

Pharaoh took a sip of his Moet, then asked "So, what do you wanna do, Ollie, 'cause you already know I'ma back ya' hand?"

"I want my own run. I want to grab my own cribs, cars and money. You feel me, my own. I want one mo' run."

"I feel you. I got a million dollars in the house, and it's yours. You earned it by keeping it all the way official when everybody else folded." Pharaoh paused for a moment, and then continued, "Ollie, whatever you get into, I don't want no parts of it, 'cause we already know the feds got it in for us. They're just waitin' on us to do anything. But if you need my help, I mean my absolute help, you know I got you."

"Thanks, P. I knew you'd understand."

"So, what are you going to do?"

"Find me a connect on some coke, and build me an army of some official niggas, then take over the city."

"Sounds like you've been plotting on this for a minute?"

"You don't even know. That was all I could think about while I was in the county. I want it so bad that I can taste it.

All I really want and need right now is <u>One</u> <u>Mo'</u> <u>Run</u>..."

Sample chapter from
Kwame: An American Hero.
Available now!

The streets are calling

Kwame's war against the most ruthless drug gang in Brownsville, led up to his one-man attack of the hardest penetrated fortress there ever was in the hood. If he could penetrate that fortress so easily by himself, he wondered how the cops could act like it didn't exist. The two men standing guard at the door didn't even see him coming. The loud thump of a punch to the throat of the 6ft-5-inch giant guarding the door with his life, had the breath taken right out of him with that one punch. He stumbled to the ground without any hope of ever getting back up. His partner noticed the swift and effective delivery of the man's punch, and thought twice about approaching him. Running would be the smartest option at this time, but how cowardice that would be? The attacker was but five feet ten inches tall and perhaps one hundred and ninety pounds in weight. The security guard didn't have time on his side and before he could contemplate his next move, the masked attacker wearing army fatigues, unloaded a kick to his groin that sent his 6ft-7inch frame bowing in pain while holding his nuts for soothing comfort.

Another blow to the temple followed, and the man was out permanently.

At first glance, Kwame didn't stand a chance against the two giants guarding the front door. One weighed just a little less than three hundred and twenty five pounds, and the other looked like an NFL lineman at three hundred and sixty pounds. However, Kwame was a trained Navy SEAL. He came home to find that the people closest to him were embroiled in a battle that threatened their livelihood daily. His sister, Jackie, became a crackhead while his mother, Janice, was a heroin addict. Two different types of drugs in one household, under the same roof, were enough to drive him crazy. Kwame didn't even recognize his sister, at first. She had aged at least twice her real age and his mother was completely unrecognizable. He left her a strong woman when he joined the Navy six years prior, but he came back to find his whole family had been under the control of drug dealers and the influence of drugs, and Kwame set out to do something about it.

The two giants at the door was just the beginning of his battle to get to the high level dealers who controlled the streets where he grew up. As he made his way down the long dark corridor, he could see women with their breasts bare and fully naked, bagging the supplies of drugs for distribution throughout the community. Swift on his feet like a fast moving kitten,

Kwame was unnoticeable. He could hear the loud voices of men talking about their plans to rack up another million dollars from the neighborhood through their drug distribution by week's end. The strong smell of ganja clouded the air as he approached the doorway to meet his nemesis. Without saying a word after setting foot in the room, he shot the first man who took notice of him right in the head. Outnumbered six-to-one, magazine clips sitting on the tables by the dozen, and loaded weapons at the reach of every person in the room, Kwame had to act fast. It was a brief standoff before the first guy reached for his 9Millimeter automatic weapon, and just like that, he found himself engulfed in a battle with flying bullets from his chest all the way down to his toes. Pandemonium broke and everybody reached for their guns at once. As Kwame rolled around on his back on the floor with a .44 Magnum in each hand, all five men were shot once in the head and each fell dead to the floor before they had a chance to discharge their weapons. The naked women ran for their lives as the barrage of gunshots sent them into a frenzy. The masked gun man dressed in Army fatigues was irrelevant to them. It was time to get the hell out of dodge to a safe place, away from the stash house. Not worried too much about the innocent women, Kwame pulled out a laundry bag and started filling it up with the stacks of money on the table. By the time he was done, he had estimated at least a couple of million dollars was confiscated for the good of the community. The back door was the quickest and safest exit without being noticed. After throwing the bag of money over a wall separating the stash house from the next house, Kwame lit his match and threw it on the gasoline track that he had poured before entering the house. The house was set ablaze and no evidence was left behind for the cops to build a case. It was one of the worst fires that Brownsville had seen in many years. No traces of human bones were left, as everything burned down to ashes by the time the New York Fire Department responded.

Kwame had been watching the house for weeks and he intended on getting rid of everything, including the people behind the big drug operation that was destroying his community. Before going to the front of the house to get rid of the security guards, he had laid out his plan to burn down the house if he couldn't get past them. A gallon of gasoline was poured in front of all the doors, except the front way where the two bouncers stood guard. His plan was to start the fire in the back and quickly rush to the front to pour out more gasoline to block every possible exit way, but that was his last option. His first option was to grab some of the money to begin his plans to finance the local community center for the neighborhood kids. His first option worked and it was on to the next house.

When Kwame came home to find his mother and sister almost a shell of what he left behind, he was determined to get rid of the bad elements in his neighborhood. Mad that he had to leave home to escape the belly of the beast, Kwame came back with a vengeance. He wanted to give every little boy and little girl in his neighborhood a chance at survival and a future. He understood that the military did him some good, but he had to work twice as hard to even get considered for the elite Navy SEALs. The military was something that he definitely didn't want any boys from his neighborhood to join. For him, it was his best option and in the end, he made the most of it. Guerilla warfare was the most precious lesson he learned while in the military, and it was those tactics that he'd planned on using to clean up his neighborhood. Kwame wanted to do it all alone. A one man show meant that only he could be the cause of his own demise. There'd be no snitches to worry about, no outside help, no betrayal and most of all, no deception from anybody. Self- reliance was one of the training tactics he also learned in the Navy and it was time for him to apply all that he learned to make his community all it could be.

Getting rid of that stash house was one of his first missions. Kwame had seen the crack houses sprouting all over the neighborhood and it would take precise planning on his part to get rid of them one by one, without getting caught by the police. Kwame also knew that he wasn't just going to be fighting the drug dealers, but some of the crooked cops that were part of the criminal enterprise plaguing the hood as well. At this point, Kwame was one up on the "Benjamins Click," one of the most dangerous drug gangs in Brownsville, Brooklyn. It was just the beginning of a long fight, but the history behind what led to this point is the most fascinating aspect of Kwame's story.

A Sample chapter from King of Detroit by Dorian Sykes

Chapter One

-1987-

I remember the last time I saw my father alive, that day will forever be stuck in my memory. We were sitting at a red light on 7 Mile and Conant with the top down on my Pop's new triple black Benz. We were listening to Frankie Beverly and Mayes, sounds pumpin', when out of nowhere a black van rammed us from behind. An old silver Chrysler pulled on the driver's side and tried boxing us in, but just as two masked gunmen exited the van, the light turned green and Pops smashed out, jumping the curb and making a hard right turn down Conant.

"Get down!" King David yelled, pushing me down.

The gunmen let off a few shots, one hitting the dashboard and another cracking the windshield. Pops lifted the top on the Benz while plotting our escape route. Seeing that the Chrysler was only a few cars behind and the van not too far behind them, Pops smashed the gas trying to get enough distance to make a turn down a side street.

"Son, listen, I am going to turn this next corner, and when I do, I want you to jump out," Pops said scanning the rearview mirror.

"I'm not leaving you," I said. My heart was racing.

"Coach, now isn't the time. I am not about to chance letting anything happen to you." Pops bent the corner doing damn near fifty, he slammed on the brakes and came to a violent stop. "Go! Go!" he yelled.

"I don't want to," I said refusing to get out of the car.

"Coach, get the fuck out of the car now!" he yelled. Pops reached over to open my door and pushed me out of the car. I landed on my side and by this time the old Chrysler and black van were bending the corner.

"Run Coach!" yelled Pops.

I hesitated because I didn't want to leave my father. Although there wasn't much I could do besides die with him, I was willing to do that.

"Got damn it Coach, run!" Pops yelled while looking back. I reluctantly got up, turned and started running. It was too late, the Chrysler had boxed Pops in and the gunmen in the van were out, guns drawn. I stopped at the corner and hid behind some bushes as I watched the men snatch Pops out of the car and drag him to the van at gun point. They threw him in the back, then sped off with the Chrysler in tow.

That was the last time I saw my father alive. And I have to live with the fact that I cost him his life by hesitating. If I had followed his instructions and just ran he would have had enough time to get away as well.

*****

"You peon muthafuckas think ya'll gone get away with snatchin' me. Do you know who the fuck I am?"

"Yeah, a dead man," one of the masked gunmen jokingly said.

"Muthafucka, I'm King David!"

"Yeah, and I'm King Tut. Why don't you just shut the fuck up and accept the fact that yo' ass 'bouts to die."

The black van pulled into the driveway of an abandoned two- family flat on the east side of Detroit. The van stopped at the side door of the house and one of the gunmen slid the door open on the van.

"Ya'll ready for this bitch?" he asked.

"Yeah, bring his ass down in the basement," a man standing in the doorway demanded.

"Come on bitch, show time."

Two gunmen snatched King David up and escorted him into the house and down into the basement. It was pitch dark down there the only light was the sun rays peeking through the dusty windows. It smelled like death down there. Needles, empty beer cans, dirty soiled mattresses, clothes, etc. cluttered the basement, giving it a musty smell. The gunmen escorted King David to a wooden chair and pushed him down in it.

"Tie his ass up," one man ordered.

Two masked men immediately began wrapping rope around KD's skinny frame.

"You lollypop ass nuccas really think ya'll gone get away with this. As soon as my man finds out I'm missin', the city will be shut down," KD snapped confidently.

"And who is your man?" asked one of the masked men.

"I'm certain you've heard of him, Dump."

"Dump? You hear this old clown nucca. He thinks Dump is going to save him." Everyone started laughing.

"So you think Dump is going to save you, huh?" asked the masked man, as he peeled off his mask, which had been muffling his voice.

King David's eyes damn near popped out his head at the sight standing before him. His entire body was filled with rage and disbelief. He couldn't believe what he was seeing. It was his right hand man, Dump. The very man he thought was going to save his life.

"Why Dump?" asked King David.

"Question is, why not?" Your time is over, been over but your bitch ass refused to pass the torch so, I'm taking it."

"What do you want" asked King David.

"What I have always wanted for you to see me as the king. I could have just had them kill you but I needed for you to know who dethroned you."

"So, what's next, Dump?"

"For you to call me King."

"I will never call you King. You are a snake and I fault myself for not seeing this coming."

"Oh, you will call me 'King Dump' one way or another. We're going to start with your fingers, one by one we're going to chop 'em off. And then we'll work on the toes and so forth. But you will honor me before you die. Grab that saw and bring it over here," ordered Dump.

One of his flunkies quickly retrieved the power saw and handed it over to Dump. The saw made a violent screeching sound as it came to life.

"You hear that?" Dump asked while squeezing the saw's trigger. "Now tell me, what's my name?" he asked while lowering the saw to King David's right foot.

"Clown," King David answered.

"Wrong answer," Dump said, then pressed the spinning blade against the bone of King David's big toe. Blood shot everywhere as Dump forced the blade through.

"Ahh…" screamed King David in agony. His big toe now sat in front of him, the bone could be seen where it was disconnected, and blood continued to spurt in all directions.

"Just think, only nine more to go," Dump taunted.

"Now let's try again. What' my name?"

"Coward!" yelled King David, as he spit in Dump's face.

"Pull his pants down," ordered Dump. "Pull 'em all the way down, his boxers too."

"What you gone do now, suck my dick!" snapped King David as he sat there exposed for all to see.

"Nah, bitch. Keith, grab his dick and hold it up."

"What?" Keith asked in disbelief, not wanting to touch another man's dick.

"Just do what the fuck I said," yelled Dump. He was getting frustrated. All he wanted was the respect of the streets. He had managed to turn Keith and a few other workers under him against King David. Keith reluctantly grabbed a hold of King David's manhood and tried not to make eye contact with him.

"That's right, Keith, do as you're told. I knew you were a spineless-snake-coward-bitch nucca. I should have killed…"

The sound of the saw and sudden pain cut King David's sentence short. I mean literally cut it short. He was in so much pain that all he could do is hope for death. Dump held King David's dick in his hand, which was now detached. He held it up in the air, and then said, "You are no longer a man. You are a bitch to the highest power," he said, then burst out into a sinister laugh.

Dump slapped King David hard across the face with his own dick. "You may never call me King, but your son lil' Coach, I will definitely be his King. Finish this bitch off," Dump ordered as he handed the saw to Keith.

Just like that, Dump crowned himself the new King. He had waited long enough for his opportunity to take over and today was that day. He exited the basement as King Dump, while his best friend and boss screamed in severe agony as Keith and the gang finished torturing him. They cut all his toes and fingers off, and severed his head, arms and legs. Dump left orders to box up King David's body parts and have them delivered to the streets in broad daylight. Dump wanted to send a clear message that he was the new King.

Serosa becomes the subject to information that could financially ruin and possibly destroy the lives and careers of many prominent people involved in the government if this data is exposed. As this intricate plot thickens, speculations start mounting and a whirlwind of death, deceit, and betrayal finds its way into the ranks of a once impenetrable core of the government. Will Serosa fall victim to the genetic structure that indirectly binds her to her parents causing her to realize there s NO WAY OUT!

In Stores!!!

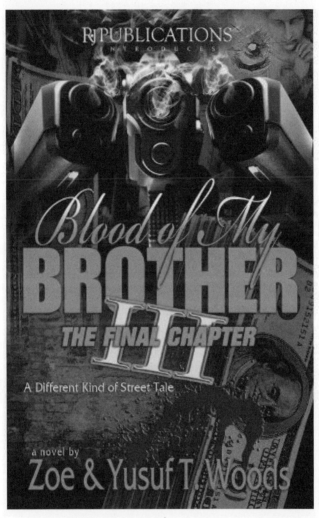

Retiring is no longer an option for Roc, who is now forced to restudy Philly's vicious streets through blood filled eyes. He realizes that his brother's killer is none other than his mentor, Mr. Holmes. With this knowledge, the strategic game of chess that began with the pushing of a pawn in the Blood of My Brother series, symbolizes one of love, loyalty, blood, mayhem, and death. In the end, the streets of Philadelphia will never be the same...

In Storess!!!

After Chasin' Satisfaction, Julius finds that satisfaction is not all that it's cracked up to be. It left nothing but death in its aftermath. Now living the glamorous life in Miami while putting the finishing touches on his hybrid condo hotel, he realizes with newfound success he's now become the hunted. Julian's success is threatened as someone from his past vows revenge on him.

In Stores!!!

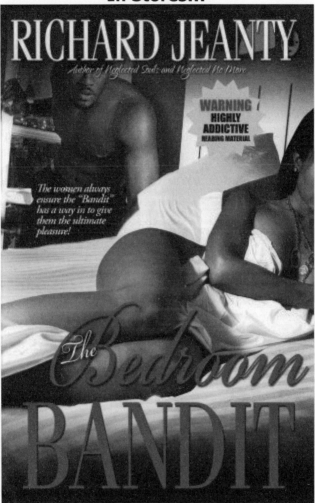

It may not be Histeria Lane, but these desperate housewives are fed up with their neglecting husbands. Their sexual needs take precedence over the millions of dollars their husbands bring home every year to keep them happy in their affluent neighborhood. While their husbands claim to be hard at work, these wives are doing a little work of their own with the bedroom bandit. Is the bandit swift enough to evade these angry husbands?

In Stores!!

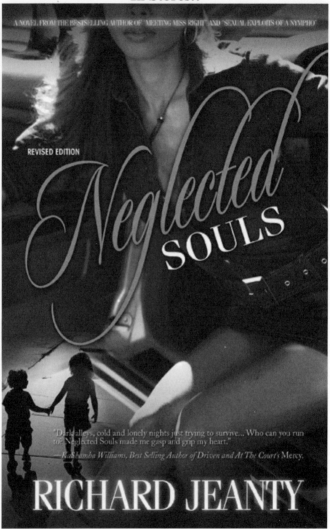

NEGLECTED SOULS

Motherhood and the trials of loving too hard and not enough frame this story...The realism of these characters will bring tears to your spirit as you discover the hero in the villain you never saw coming...

In Stores!!!

Jimmy and Nina continue to feel a void in their lives because they haven't a clue about their genealogical make-up. Jimmy falls victims to a life threatening illness and only the right organ donor can save his life. Will the donor be the bridge to reconnect Jimmy and Nina to their biological family? Will Nina be the strength for her brother in his time of need? Will they ever find out what really happened to their mother?

In Stores!!!

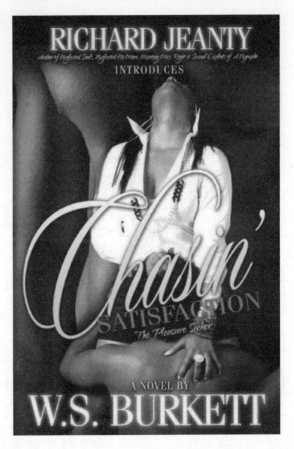

Betrayal, lust, lies, murder, deception, sex and tainted love frame this story... Julian Stevens lacks the ambition and freak ability that Miko looks for in a man, but she married him despite his flaws to spite an ex-boyfriend. When Miko least expects it, the old boyfriend shows up and ready to sweep her off her feet again. She wants to have her cake and eat it too. While Miko's doing her own thing, Julian is determined to become everything Miko ever wanted in a man and more, but will he go to extreme lengths to prove he's worthy of Miko's love? Julian Stevens soon finds out that he's capable of being more than he could ever imagine as he embarks on a journey that will change his life forever.

In Stores!!!

The police in New York and other major cities around the country are increasingly victimizing black men. The violence has escalated to deadly force, most of the time without justification. In this controversial book, noted author Richard Jeanty, tackles the problem of police brutality and the unfair treatment of Black men at the hands of police in New York City and the rest of the country.

In Stores!!!

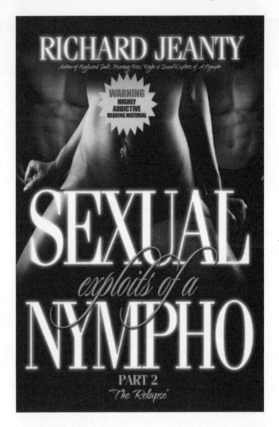

Just when Darren thinks his relationship with Tina is flourishing, there is yet another hurdle on the road hindering their bliss. Tina saw a therapist for months to deal with her sexual addiction, but now Darren is wondering if she was ever treated completely. Darren has not been taking care of home and Tina's frustrated and agrees to a break-up with Darren. Will Darren lose Tina for good? Will Tina ever realize that Darren is the best man for her?

In Stores!!

Ronald Murphy was a player all his life until he and his best friend, Myles, met the women of their dreams during a brief vacation in South Beach, Florida. Sexual Jeopardy is story of trust, betrayal, forgiveness, friendship and hope.

In Stores!!!

Tina develops an insatiable sexual appetite very early in life. She only loves her boyfriend, Darren, but he's too far away in college to satisfy her sexual needs.

Tina decides to get buck wild away in college

Will her sexual trysts jeopardize the lives of the men in her life?

In Stores!!!

Faith Jones, a woman in her mid-thirties, has given up on ever finding love again until she met her son's best friend, Darius. Faith Jones is walking a thin line of betrayal against her son for the love of Darius. Will Faith allow her emotions to outweigh her common sense?

In Stores!!!

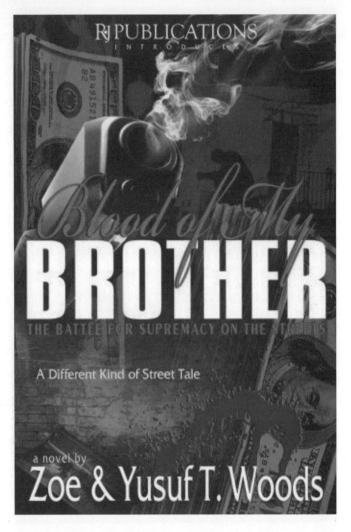

Roc was the man on the streets of Philadelphia, until his younger brother decided it was time to become his own man by wreaking havoc on Roc's crew without any regards for the blood relation they share. Drug, murder, mayhem and the pursuit of happiness can lead to deadly consequences. This story can only be told by a person who has lived it.

In Stores!!!

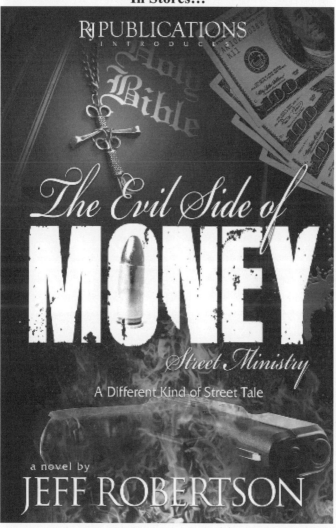

Violence, Intimidation and carnage are the order as Nathan and his brother set out to build the most powerful drug empires in Chicago. However, when God comes knocking, Nathan's conscience starts to surface. Will his haunted criminal past get the best of him?

In Stores!!

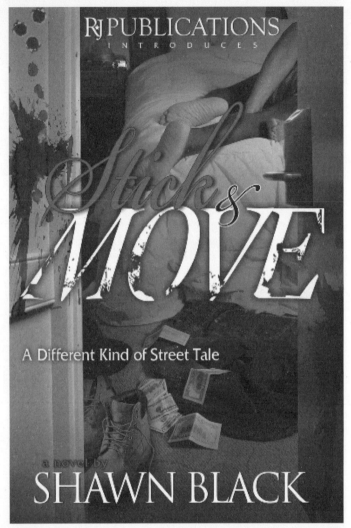

Yasmina witnessed the brutal murder of her parents at a young age at the hand of a drug dealer. This event stained her mind and upbringing as a result. Will Yamina's life come full circle with her past? Find out as Yasmina's crew, The Platinum Chicks, set out to make a name for themselves on the street.

In stores!!

Ashland's mother, Bianca, fights hard to suppress the truth from her daughter because she doesn't want her to marry Jordan, the grandson of an ex-lover she loathes. Ashland soon finds out how cruel and vengeful her mother can be, but what price will Bianca pay for redemption?

In stores!!

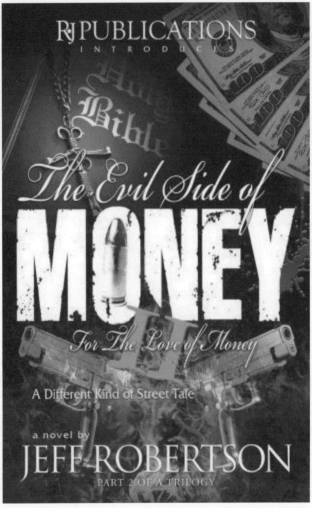

A beautigul woman from Bolivia threatens the existence of the drug empire that Nate and G have built. While Nate is head over heels for her, G can see right through her. As she brings on more conflict between the crew, G sets out to show Nate exactly who she is before she brings about their demise.

In Stores!!!

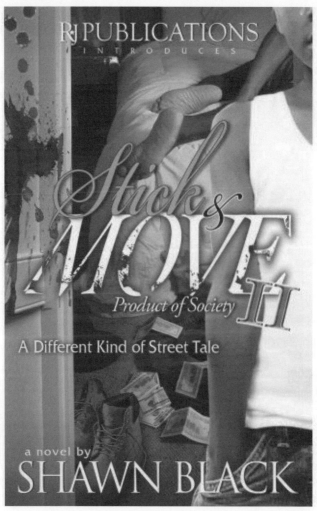

Scorcher and Yasmina's low key lifestyle was interrupted when they were taken down by the Feds, but their daughter, Serosa, was left to be raised by the foster care system. Will Serosa become a product of her environment or will she rise above it all? Her bloodline is undeniable, but will she be able to control it?

In Stores!!

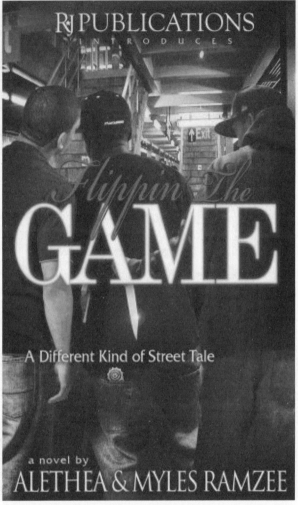

An ex-drug dealer finds himself in a bind after he's caught by the Feds. He has to decide which is more important, his family or his loyalty to the game. As he fights hard to make a decision, those who helped him to the top fear the worse from him. Will he get the chance to tell the govt. whole story, or will someone get to him before he becomes a snitch?

In Stores!!!

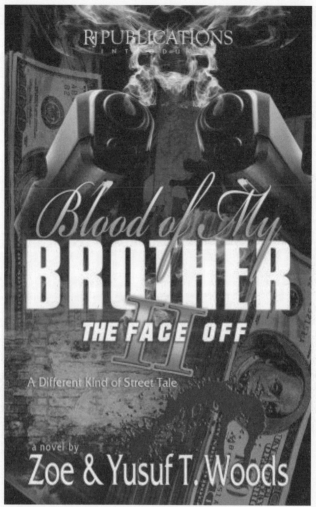

What will Roc do when he finds out the true identity of Solo? Will the blood shed come from his own brother Lil Mac? Will Roc and Solo take their beef to an explosive height on the street? Find out as Zoe and Yusuf bring the second installment to their hot street joint, Blood of My Brother.

In Stores!!!

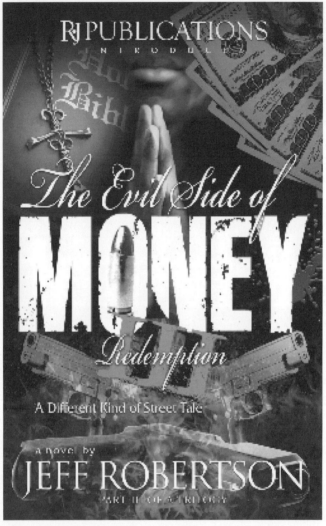

Forced to abandon the drug world for good, Nathan and G attempt to change their lives and move forward, but will their past come back to haunt them? This final installment will leave you speechless.

In Stores!!!

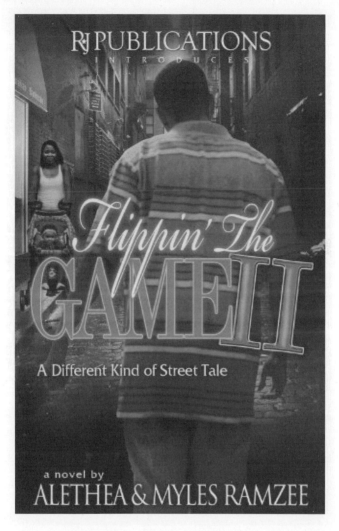

Nafiys Muhammad managed to beat the charges in court and was found innocent as a result. However, his criminal involvement is far from over. While Jerry Class Classon is feeling safe in the witness protection program, his family continues to endure even more pain. There will be many revelations as betrayal, sex scandal, corruption, and murder shape this story. No one will be left unscathed and everyone will pay the price for his/her involvement. Get ready for a rough ride as we revisit the Black Top Crew.

In Stores!!

Dave Richardson is enjoying success as his second book became a New York Times best-seller. He left the life of The Bedroom behind to settle with his family, but an obsessed fan has not had enough of Dave and she will go to great length to get a piece of him. How far will a woman go to get a man that doesn't belong to her?

In Stores!!!

Deon is at the mercy of a ruthless gang that kidnapped him. In a foreign land where he knows nothing about the culture, he has to use his survival instincts and his wit to outsmart his captors. Will the Hoodfellas show up in time to rescue Deon, or will Crazy D take over once again and fight an all out war by himself?

In Stores!!!

The drama continues as Deshun is hunted by Angela who still feels that ex-girlfriend Kayla is still trying to win his heart, though he brutally raped her. Angela will kill anyone who gets in her way, but is DeShun worth all the aggravation?

In Stores!!!

Buck Johnson was forced to make the best out of worst situation. He has witnessed the most cruel events in his life and it is those events who the man that he has become. Was the Johnson family ignorant souls through no fault of their own?

In Stores!!!

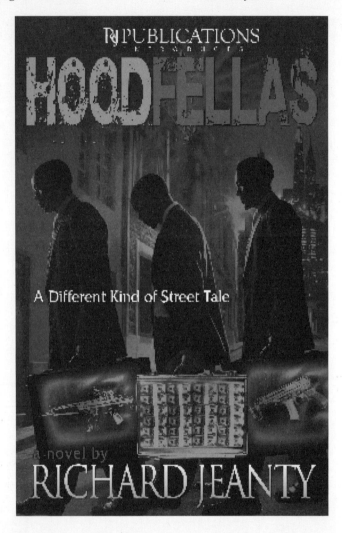

When an Ex-con finds himself destitute and in dire need of the basic necessities after he's released from prison, he turns to what he knows best, crime, but at what cost? Extortion, murder and mayhem drives him back to the top, but will he stay there?

In Stores !!!

What happens when someone falls insanely in love? Stalking is just the beginning.

In Stores!!!

Pharaoh decides that his fate would not be settled in court by twelve jurors. His fate would be decided in blood, as he sets out to kill Tez, and those who snitched on him. Pharaoh s definition of Going All Out is either death or freedom. Prison is not an option. Will Pharoah impose his will on those snitches?

In Stores 10/30/2011

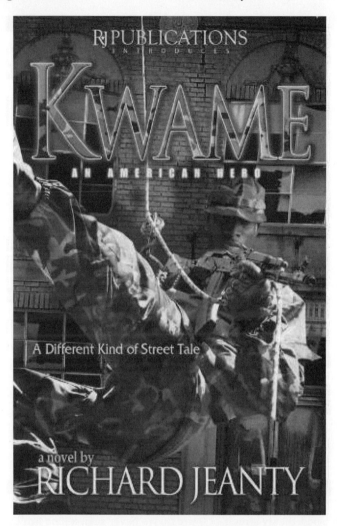

Kwame never thought he would come home to find his mother and sister strung out on drugs after his second tour of duty in Iraq. Kwame wanted to come back home to lead a normal life. However, Dirty cops and politicians alike refuse to clean the streets of Newark, New Jersey because the drug industry is big business that keeps their pockets fat. Kwame is determined to rid his neighborhood of all the bad elements, including the dirty cops, dirty politicians and the drug dealers. Will his one man army be enough for the job?
IN STORES NOW!!

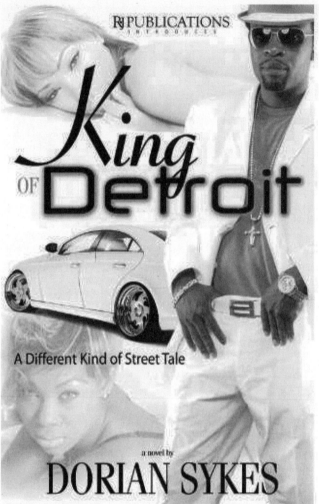

The blood-thirsty streets of Detroit have never seen a King like Corey Coach Townsend. The Legacy of Corey Coach Townsend, the Real King of Detroit, will live on forever. Coach was crowned King after avenging his father s murder, and after going to war with his best friend over the top spot. He always keeps his friends close. Coach s reign as king will forever be stained in the streets of Detroit, as the best who had ever done it, but how will he rise to the top? This is a story of betrayal, revenge and honor. There can only be one king!

In Stores February 15, 2012

PUBLICATIONS
BRINGING EXCITEMENT, FUN AND JOY TO READING

Use this coupon to order by mail

1. Neglected Souls, Richard Jeanty $14.95 Available
2. Neglected No More, Richard Jeanty $14.95Available
3. Ignorant Souls, Richard Jeanty $15.00, Available
4. Sexual Exploits of Nympho, Richard Jeanty $14.95 Available
5. Meeting Ms. Right's Whip Appeal, Richard Jeanty $14.95 Available
6. Me and Mrs. Jones, K.M Thompson $14.95 Available
7. Chasin' Satisfaction, W.S Burkett $14.95 Available
8. Extreme Circumstances, Cereka Cook $14.95 Available
9. The Most Dangerous Gang In America, R. Jeanty $15.00 Available
10. Sexual Exploits of a Nympho II, Richard Jeanty $15.00 Available
11. Sexual Jeopardy, Richard Jeanty $14.95 Available
12. Too Many Secrets, Too Many Lies, Sonya Sparks $15.00 Available
13. Stick And Move, Shawn Black $15.00 Available
14. Evil Side Of Money, Jeff Robertson $15.00 Available
15. Evil Side Of Money II, Jeff Robertson $15.00 Available
16. Evil Side Of Money III, Jeff Robertson $15.00 Available
17. Flippin' The Game, Alethea and M. Ramzee, $15.00 Available
18. Flippin' The Game II, Alethea and M. Ramzee, $15.00 Available
19. Cater To Her, W.S Burkett $15.00 Available
20. Blood of My Brother I, Zoe & Yusuf Woods $15.00 Available
21. Blood of my Brother II, Zoe & Ysuf Woods $15.00 Available
22. Hoodfellas, Richard Jeanty $15.00 available
23. Hoodfellas II, Richard Jeanty, $15.00 03/30/2010
24. The Bedroom Bandit, Richard Jeanty $15.00 Available
25. Mr. Erotica, Richard Jeanty, $15.00, Sept 2010
26. Stick N Move II, Shawn Black $15.00 Available
27. Stick N Move III, Shawn Black $15.00 Available
28. Miami Noire, W.S. Burkett $15.00 Available
29. Insanely In Love, Cereka Cook $15.00 Available
30. Blood of My Brother III, Zoe & Yusuf Woods Available
31. Mr. Erotica
32. My Partner's Wife
33. Deceived I
34. Deceived II
35. Going All Out I
36. Going All Out II 10/30/2011
37. Kwame 12/15/2011
38. King of Detroit 2/15/2012

Name_____
Address_____
City_____State_____Zip Code_____

Please send the novels that I have circled above.

Shipping and Handling: Free

Total Number of Books_____Total Amount Due_____

Buy 3 books and get 1 free. Send institution check or money order (no cash or CODs) to: RJ Publication: PO Box 300310, Jamaica, NY 11434

For info. call 718-471-2926, or www.rjpublications.com Please allow 2-3 weeks for delivery.

Use this coupon to order by mail

39. Neglected Souls, Richard Jeanty $14.95 Available
40. Neglected No More, Richard Jeanty $14.95 Available
41. Ignorant Souls, Richard Jeanty $15.00, Available
42. Sexual Exploits of Nympho, Richard Jeanty $14.95 Available
43. Meeting Ms. Right's Whip Appeal, Richard Jeanty $14.95 Available
44. Me and Mrs. Jones, K.M Thompson $14.95 Available
45. Chasin' Satisfaction, W.S Burkett $14.95 Available
46. Extreme Circumstances, Cereka Cook $14.95 Available
47. The Most Dangerous Gang In America, R. Jeanty $15.00 Available
48. Sexual Exploits of a Nympho II, Richard Jeanty $15.00 Available
49. Sexual Jeopardy, Richard Jeanty $14.95 Available
50. Too Many Secrets, Too Many Lies, Sonya Sparks $15.00 Available
51. Stick And Move, Shawn Black $15.00 Available
52. Evil Side Of Money, Jeff Robertson $15.00 Available
53. Evil Side Of Money II, Jeff Robertson $15.00 Available
54. Evil Side Of Money III, Jeff Robertson $15.00 Available
55. Flippin' The Game, Alethea and M. Ramzee, $15.00 Available
56. Flippin' The Game II, Alethea and M. Ramzee, $15.00 Available
57. Cater To Her, W.S Burkett $15.00 Available
58. Blood of My Brother I, Zoe & Yusuf Woods $15.00 Available
59. Blood of my Brother II, Zoe & Ysuf Woods $15.00 Available
60. Hoodfellas, Richard Jeanty $15.00 available
61. Hoodfellas II, Richard Jeanty, $15.00 03/30/2010
62. The Bedroom Bandit, Richard Jeanty $15.00 Available
63. Mr. Erotica, Richard Jeanty, $15.00, Sept 2010
64. Stick N Move II, Shawn Black $15.00 Available
65. Stick N Move III, Shawn Black $15.00 Available
66. Miami Noire, W.S. Burkett $15.00 Available
67. Insanely In Love, Cereka Cook $15.00 Available
68. Blood of My Brother III, Zoe & Yusuf Woods Available
69. Mr. Erotica
70. My Partner's Wife
71. Deceived 1/15/2011
72. Going All Out 2/15/2011

Name_____
Address_____
City_____State_____Zip Code_____

Please send the novels that I have circled above.
Shipping and Handling: Free
Total Number of Books_____Total Amount Due_____
         Buy 3 books and get 1 free. This offer is subject to change without notice.
Send institution check or money order (no cash or CODs) to:
RJ Publications
PO Box 300310
Jamaica, NY 11434
For more information please call 718-471-2926, or visit www.rjpublications.com
Please allow 2-3 weeks for delivery.